"Was there anything unusual about this trip?" beautiful Inspector Bingham asked. "Did you notice anything different from the other three?"

He considered.

"They were more serious," he said. "About the birdwatching like. On the other trips there were one or two fanatics, but most were there to have a good time. They wanted to see the birds, but if they didn't, it wouldn't be the end of the world. On this one you felt it was a matter, well, of life and death. . . ."

Also by Ann Cleeves
Published by Fawcett Books:

A BIRD IN THE HAND
COME DEATH AND HIGH WATER
A LESSON IN DYING
MURDER IN PARADISE
A PREY TO MURDER
MURDER IN MY BACKYARD

SEA FEVER

Ann Cleeves

FAWCETT GOLD MEDAL • NEW YORK

A Fawcett Gold Medal Book
Published by Ballantine Books
Copyright © 1991 By Ann Cleeves

All rights reserved under International and Pan-American Copyright Conventions. Published in the United States by Ballantine Books, a division of Random House, Inc., New York and simultaneously in Canada by Random House of Canada Limited, Toronto.

Library of Congress Catalog Card Number: 91-91984

ISBN: 0-449-14707-X

Manufactured in the United States of America

First Edition: October 1991

1

Even if there had been no murder, the last trip of the season of the *Jessie Ellen* would have been news. A new bird for the world, after all, is rather special. There would undoubtedly have been interviews with specialist reporters, speculation about where the bird could possibly breed, sponsorship, perhaps, for an expedition to track it down to a cliff in some lonely and uninhabited island. There was, George felt all along, a relationship between the murder of the boy and the sighting of a storm petrel never before recorded. He was not so superstitious that he considered the death as a cause of the appearance of the bird. It was no sacrifice to the forces of nature. Neither did he see the petrel as an albatross bringing misfortune and disaster with its astounding beauty. Yet he thought that if the bird had never appeared, flying so close to the boat that they could make a plan of its wing formula and see the colour of the webs of its feet, Greg Franks would still be alive. Certainly the boy's death spoiled the bird for them. They hated him, as if it were his fault, because the elation and joy which should have lasted for weeks was cut short, and the fame they deserved was denied to them.

George Palmer-Jones met Greg Franks first at Holywell Pond, a Northumberland Wildlife Trust Reserve. The memory of the meeting was strangely vivid, though there had been many such incidents in his birdwatching career. Afterwards, when other rare birds turned up, he looked out for

1

Greg and noticed him. Despite that, when Mr. and Mrs. Franks hired him to trace their missing son, he did not at first connect them with the boy who had disturbed the Baillon's crake at Holywell. When he did, the memory of the day returned to him sharp and complete, as if it had happened only minutes before.

It had been early June, a hot and sticky day with the threat of thunder and swallows flying low over yellow rape fields. The field by the pond was waist-high with buttercups, clover, and cow parsley. George arrived at the hide overlooking the pond at lunchtime, to discover that the bird had not been seen that day. It was probably skulking in the reed bed, said the exultant locals who had found the bird. It often did that.

The hide was full of people crammed together along the bench seat, waiting. There was the smell of hot creosote and damp vegetation. They talked occasionally, but their attention was on the still water. They were prepared to wait until evening. "Just be patient," said the locals. "It came out at dusk yesterday. It won't have gone anywhere."

Then Greg Franks burst into the hide. He seemed physically incapable of patience. He paced across the wooden floor smoking one cigarette after another, and his restlessness was so obvious, so flamboyant, that he unsettled all the others there.

"I want some action," he said at last. "I'm going in. I need this bird."

"Don't be a fool, man," said one of the locals, a big square man with hands like spades. "You'll scare it off; then no one will see it. This is a nature reserve. Do you think the trust will put out news of other rarities if you go tramping all over it?"

He stood up to confront Greg, blocking his way, and George thought there might be a fight. But Greg was too quick for them. He slipped out of the hide and into the reserve. They saw his sleek black head moving like a stoat's through the reed bed. A moorhen gave an alarm call and splashed into view. In the hide there was silence.

Suddenly the crake was in the open, flying. It was so close to the hide that they could not focus their binoculars onto it.

The bird flew around the pond once more, and they thought it would settle again at the edge of the water to give more prolonged views, but it changed direction and disappeared very quickly in the heat haze. Greg Franks must have tripped in the reed bed, because when he stood up to wave his arms triumphantly at them, he was dripping wet, and his hair straggled like seaweed across his face.

When he returned to the hide, George was surprised by the reception the boy received. The bird had been frightened off by an act of stupid exhibitionism, yet the watchers were indulgent, as if George were a spoilt but gifted child who should be allowed his own way. They had, of course, obtained brilliant if fleeting views of the bird. The birdwatchers who arrived later in the afternoon were less understanding and threatened unimaginable tortures to Franks if they should catch him.

In the following year George Palmer-Jones saw Greg Franks several times. He was on Scilly for most of October and seemed suddenly to be at every new bird. Recently, George saw, he had taken to driving a maroon Mercedes with American numberplates.

He usually had a group of friends with him—wild young men like himself and pretty girls. There were rumours that he made his money through drug dealing or theft or some vaguely illegal deals with friends in the city. He always seemed to have money, and he was always one of the first to arrive at a rarity, but no one seemed too concerned about what lay behind his apparent affluence. Birdwatching is full of eccentrics. They were more interested in his list.

The subject of Greg Franks' list was brought up wherever the more avid twitchers gathered together. It must be immense, they said. Now he went for everything. Surely it must rival the older twitchers who had those blockers from the sixties. Surely by now it must be as big as Roger Pym's.

George was not one of those for whom the speculation about lists is as important as seeing the birds themselves, and when he and his wife were hired by Mr. and Mrs. Franks to trace their missing son, he made no connection with Greg.

It was more than a year after the visit to Holywell Pond. The first contact was by phone, and George took the call.

"Yes," he said. "Palmer-Jones."

The woman on the other end of the phone had a Bristol accent, and her voice was breathless and shaking with nerves.

"That is Mr. Palmer-Jones, the private detective?" she insisted.

He hated the term, but she was so anxious already that he only said, "How can I help you?"

Then, in an incoherent stream of words, she pleaded with him to visit her and Mr. Franks at home. They were desperate, and the problem was too difficult, she said, too personal, to discuss on the telephone. It was midsummer, a quiet time for work and for birding, and George agreed to go to see them.

They found the house on a long and busy road in a soulless Bristol suburb close to the Rolls-Royce factory. George's wife, Molly, was driving. It was a dual carriageway, with a motorway roundabout at one end and a bus station at the other. The house was mock Tudor, semidetached, with leaded windows and black beams on the gables. In a quiet cul-de-sac it might have been considered a desirable place to live, but with the lorries thundering past the wrought iron gates, it seemed desolate, stranded in a treeless no-man's land.

The Franks must have been waiting for them, because the door opened immediately. Molly reached the house first because the driver's seat was next to the pavement, and George had to wait for a break in the traffic before he dared leave the car; yet the man inside looked past her, as if she were invisible or not worth speaking to.

"Mr. Palmer-Jones," he said. The Bristol accent was unusually hard and rather high-pitched. "It was good of you to come."

He had to shout against the traffic noise. He gestured for them to enter the house, then shut the door firmly behind them. They stood uncertainly in a dark hall. He was a small, solid, vigourous man. Despite the heat he wore a long cardigan over a sticky nylon shirt. In the background Mrs. Franks hovered fussily. Dennis Franks did not introduce her.

4

"Come into the lounge," he said, still directing his words to George. "I expect you'd like some tea." He turned to his wife. "Tea!" he said, and she disappeared through the kitchen door.

The living room was square, with a bay window which looked out over the main road. As they talked, the roar of the traffic outside filled the silences in their conversation. It was late August and hot, but none of the windows were open. The bright sunshine was filtered through net curtains, so everything seemed rather overcast and dusty. Every available surface was covered with china and glass ornaments, vases of silk flowers, framed photographs, so it seemed to George that there was hardly room to move.

"It was good of you to come," Dennis Franks repeated. "My wife thought you might not understand over the telephone. I decided it would be better to ask you to come here."

George felt stifled and trapped. There were better places to be in the last week of August. In the valleys of south-west Cornwall the first autumn migrants would be arriving. He should be planning his usual bank holiday birding weekend in Norfolk.

"What is the problem, precisely?" he asked, facing his attention back to the room. "You'd like us to trace your son?"

"That's right!" The man's voice was sharp and irritable. "He's been missing for months. We hear about him occasionally, and sometimes he phones up to tell his mother he's all right, but he moves around a lot, and we never know where he is."

"Is there any special reason for wanting to trace him now?" George asked.

"It was Muriel's idea," Franks said angrily. "She thought it was the right thing to do. I want to sell the business, and she thinks the lad should be consulted before I go ahead. I told her there's no chance that he'd want to come back here and work for the family. He made that quite clear when he left home. I'm not sure what she's doing. I think it's only an excuse to get him home. She misses him."

He spoke as if this were some unaccountable weakness. Molly watched him curiously.

"What is your business?" she asked, and realised at once that it had been the right question. He spoke to her directly for the first time.

"Franks' Meat Products," the man said with pride. "We make sausage skins. They're famous in the trade. I've been offered a very good price."

"Who advised you to contact us?" George asked. Before his retirement he had worked as a civil servant with the Home Office. More recently he and his wife had started an enquiry agency. They were based in Surrey, and though they received referrals occasionally from solicitors in other parts of the country, it was unusual to be contacted by an unknown member of the public. They never advertised their services.

"No one advised me," Franks said. He seemed surprised. "I heard about you from Gregory, of course, when he was still at home. You're a birdwatcher, aren't you? You must have heard of our Gregory. I understand that he's something of a celebrity in his own field."

"Of course," George said. "Greg Franks. Yes, of course."

And he was taken back immediately to the hide in Northumberland, and the memory of the incident with the Baillon's crake returned to him with astonishing clarity.

He was still absorbed in the daydream when Muriel Franks came in carrying a tray. She was small, nervous, sharp-featured, quite determined, it seemed, that she would get her own way.

"You will help us find Gregory, won't you Mr. Palmer-Jones?" she said.

"I don't think there'll be any trouble at all," he said. He wanted to reassure her. She seemed so tense that he was afraid she might make a scene. "You see," he continued, speaking gently, hoping to calm her, "any of the younger birdwatchers will have his phone number. I'm sure I can put you in touch with someone who will know where he is. If I'd realised when you telephoned who your son is, I would have been able to help you then. You don't need us to do it."

He was wondering how much he could charge Franks for his wasted day.

6

"Oh, no," Muriel said so violently that he realised the obsession with her son was a desperation. She did not really want to consult Greg about the family business. She was not even concerned for his safety. She just wanted him home with her. "That won't do at all. You must see Gregory. Personally." And then, as if reading George's mind, she added, "We don't care what it costs. Do we, Dennis?" There were already tears in her eyes.

Her husband shrugged uneasily. Molly was surprised that he said so little. Perhaps he was fond of her and did not like to see her unhappy. Perhaps this independence was such a surprise to him that he did not know how to handle it.

"You must persuade Gregory to come home," Mrs. Franks continued. She spoke very quickly. "Then we can discuss the sale of the business properly. We couldn't do that over the phone. He wouldn't take us seriously. He never does."

She looked at her husband for support, but he turned away, as if embarrassed that she made her wishes so obvious. There was an awkward silence.

"Have you any other children?" Molly asked.

Muriel Franks shook her head violently.

"No," she said. "Only Gregory." She hesitated, and George was afraid she would cry again. "We were lucky to keep him," she said at last. "He was a sickly baby. He spent most of his first year in Frenchay Hospital. Perhaps that's why he's always been so special."

Molly spoke gently. "If Gregory hasn't come home of his own accord," she said, "I don't think anything we say could persuade him. You'd been wasting your money."

"You don't understand," Muriel Franks interrupted eagerly. "That's why we asked you to come here. Mr. Palmer-Jones has been a hero of Gregory's since he was a little boy. I remember him saying, when he was still at home, 'George Palmer-Jones is the only member of the British Birds Rarity Committee you can really trust. He knows more about bird identification than any man in Europe.' " She turned to her husband, her eyes bright, her voice brittle with hope. "He used to say that, didn't he, Dennis? All the time?"

The father nodded in sad agreement. Outside, the traffic rumbled past, and Molly thought that Muriel could not have been an easy woman to live with. Perhaps her husband's cold autocracy was his only means of survival.

Muriel Franks turned back to George. "If you were to go and see Greg and ask him, he'd come back. I'm sure he would."

George looked helplessly at Molly. Mrs. Franks' determination to keep her son at home was unnatural, he thought. Greg was in his early twenties, no longer a child. She was balanced precariously between elation and depression. He was frightened of saying something which would tip her into some kind of breakdown. Throughout the exchange Dennis Franks looked on anxiously. Occasionally he reached out towards his wife, as if he was going to pat her hand to calm her, but he seemed almost frightened of touching her. He stared at George without giving any indication of what he wanted the man to say.

"I don't know that I could be so persuasive," George said at last.

"You could!" Muriel cried. "Tell him that if we decide to sell the business, a share of the profit would be his. Of course all our money will go to him in the end, but we could make something available to him now. But we need him here to discuss it."

Molly thought that the purchase of her son's affection was a strategy she must have tried before. Molly and George looked at one another, each hoping the other would have the courage to disappoint the woman. There was a strained silence, which Muriel Franks took suddenly and irrationally as consent to her plans. She leapt to her feet, her face flushed with triumph.

"I knew I could make you understand if you came here and met us," she said. "You don't know what this means to me. I don't think I could carry on without the hope that I might see Greg again soon."

Then George knew that the decision had been made for him, and that he would find it impossible to refuse the work. Dennis Franks looked on with silent bewilderment and pain.

8

Muriel remained standing, as if she expected them to leave at once to find her son. She had expected immediate and dramatic action. Molly looked at her with concern.

"We'll need to know a little more about Gregory," she said. "When did he first leave home?"

Perhaps they could help, she thought, just by allowing the woman to talk about her son. Perhaps that was more important than persuading Greg that he should show her a little consideration by visiting her occasionally and letting her know where he was staying.

Muriel returned reluctantly to her seat. "I don't know," she said. "Not exactly. About twelve months ago. He's phoned since then, but he's not been back to stay."

Dennis came to her rescue. "He was always hard to keep at home," he said. "Even as a lad."

"Has he ever been in trouble with the police?" Molly asked.

"He was charged once," Franks said. "It was soon after he'd left school. We didn't find out until later. We thought he'd disappeared on one of his birdwatching trips. He was in a bail hostel in the city. But he was found not guilty in the Crown Court. He hasn't got a criminal record."

"What was he charged with?"

"Burglary," Franks said. "He was supposed to have broken into a house."

"It was all lies," Muriel Franks interrupted. "The case was thrown out. He should have come to us and told us all about it. We would have understood. We always did. We only found out he'd been in court because there was a fire in the hostel, and Greg's picture was in the paper. He was a hero. He saved someone."

She seemed about to launch into the details of Greg's heroism, but, with one of her sudden swings of mood, changed her mind.

"All this isn't important!" she said impatiently. "I can tell you exactly where Greg will be this weekend. You should be getting ready to meet him, not talking about the past." She sprang once again to her feet. "A letter came here a while ago by mistake," she said. "It wasn't personal—I

9

wouldn't ever open his personal mail—but I thought it might give me some idea where he was. I knew it would be useful. I'll get it for you!'' She hurried from the room.

Dennis Franks moved uneasily in his chair. On the road outside there was the squeal of brakes and the sound of a horn.

''I don't know what to do for the best,'' he said. ''She's set her heart on seeing him. I know he'll not stay, but when he comes, he always puts on a big show—brings her flowers and that—so he makes her happy for a while. I'm afraid she's made herself ill. She's always been wrapped up in him. Perhaps when I retire, I'll be able to help her more. . . . It's a difficult age for a woman. . . .''

He coughed a small, embarrassed cough, and they waited for Muriel Franks to return.

She rushed back into the room, breathless and eager, waving a folded piece of white paper. In the other hand was a brown envelope. She handed the paper to George, who read it carefully. The letter was a receipt and confirmation of booking. It was from a travel agency which specialised in natural history and birdwatching, based in Bristol. It said that a place had been reserved for Gregory Franks on the pelagic trip which would leave Heanor on August 27th. Accommodation had been booked at Myrtle Cottage at Porthkennan for the remainder of the week. It was signed by Rob Earl, the agency's resident ornithologist.

''I didn't understand it,'' Muriel Franks said. ''What is a pelagic trip anyway?''

''*Pelagic* is an American expression,'' George said, ''It's a boat trip especially organised to allow birdwatchers the best possible views of rare seabirds.''

But as he spoke, he was staring at the letter like a boy at a forbidden box of matches. It was a temptation. Of all birds he loved seabirds best. To George, a child brought up in the Midlands, they had represented the freedom of seaside holidays. Now he was drawn by the mystery of their life at sea. There was a challenge to find out more about them.

''Will you go?'' Muriel Franks demanded. ''We'll pay all your expenses. Will you go to Cornwall to talk to Gregory?''

10

In the stifling room, surrounded by traffic noise, in the company of these unhappy people, Cornwall was suddenly irresistible. George knew he should wait, discuss the thing with Molly, that to go would only encourage a neurotic woman in her fantasies, but he could not help himself.

"Yes," he said, trying to sound as if the decision had been a difficult one to make. "Yes, we'll go."

Rob Earl was fast asleep, dreaming of teeming Wilson's petrels and shearwaters as big as vultures which flew so close to him that he could reach out his hand and feel the rush of wind as they passed. He was in his office, leaning back in his chair with his feet on his desk. He had come to work with a hangover. The night before, he and his boss had become stupendously drunk. When his boss had offered to take him out for a drink, he had been afraid that it was to give him the sack. It seemed a luxury for a provincial chain of travel agents, even one specially involved with birdwatchers, to employ a resident ornithologist. In fact, it was to tell Rob that the agency was being bought out by a Bristol businessman. "We need fresh capital," he had said in an attempt to persuade himself and Rob that the move was a positive one. "He's promised me there'll be no major changes. We'll be able to expand. That must compensate for any loss of independence."

Yet despite his words he drank with a depressed and determined ferocity, and Rob felt obliged to keep up with him. He had no idea what the change of organisation would mean to him, but his boss wanted to buy him drinks, and he was prepared to drink them. They ended up in a scruffy old pub at the top of Cromwell Road, and Rob could not remember walking home.

As he spent the morning answering the phone and checking airline timetables, he supposed he was getting too old for such excess. At lunchtime he shut his office door, took his phone off the hook, and went to sleep.

He woke to the sound of his secretary next door, banging inexpertly at a typewriter. Laura was employed under the youth training scheme. Rob frowned. It was not only that the

11

noise irritated his hangover. He cared about his work. It offended him to send letters thick with Liquid Paper to his customers. He needed a break, he thought. He had spent too long in the office. He looked forward to a week in Cornwall. He began to drowse again, when he heard Laura talking. There were other voices which he recognised, and he wondered for an instant if he was dreaming again.

"George!" he shouted through the closed door. "What are you doing here? Where are you going? Have those bloody Cornish birders been suppressing again? Why are you the only foreigner they're prepared to talk to?"

The door opened, and George and Molly walked into the office. George looked at the recumbent figure behind the desk. Permanent employment had failed to give Rob Earl an air of respectability. He was unshaven, hollow-eyed. Molly had always liked him but thought he was reckless and a little dangerous.

"You're getting paranoid. It's nothing to do with the birds." George spoke sternly, perhaps because he needed to convince himself that he was there strictly on business. By his side Molly stood quietly, discreetly disapproving. She thought there were other ways of helping Muriel Franks than to drive to Porthkennan. In the car there had been an argument. "At least it's only indirectly to do with birds. We want your help. And perhaps the Cornish birders tell me about rare birds because I don't call them 'bloody Corns.' "

Laura had begun to type again. Rob looked at his watch. "The pubs are open," he said. "Let's have a drink, and you can tell me all about it. I haven't got long. I'm going to Porthkennan to stay with Rose Pengelly this afternoon."

"We haven't time for a drink," George said. "And I know about Porthkennan. We're here on business. We need to talk to Greg Franks. You *are* still expecting him on the pelagic you've organised?"

Rob rummaged through the papers on his desk and pulled out a typed list. "Yes," he said. "He confirmed the booking last week."

He looked up at George and smiled. Molly thought again that he was dangerous. "Why don't you come with us,

12

George?'' he said. His voice was quiet and persuasive. ''There's nothing more exciting than seawatching, nothing in the world. There's a spare place on the boat and plenty of room at Rose Pengelly's. You still need Wilson's petrel, don't you, George? People on the last three pelagics I've organised have had brilliant views. Then we'll spend the rest of the week in Cornwall with the first migrants coming in, and regular trips to Porthkennan Head for the seawatching if the weather blows up. If it's business, why don't you put it down as expenses? Claim it back from the taxman.''

Since the meeting with the Franks, George had been thinking of Cornwall as a vague, wistful dream of deep valleys and salt west wind. He knew it was romantic folly, a reaction to the hot summer spent inland. He knew Molly thought he was being weak and unprincipled.

''We'll just talk to Greg,'' he had told her in the car. ''We'll just stay one night, then come home. You can tell him how depressed his mother is. Then it'll all be over.''

Now Rob's words made the promise seem rash. He did need Wilson's petrel. And what, after all, was wrong with taking a few days off for some seawatching?

''You make a commission on every place you sell, do you?'' he said, unwilling to give in immediately.

Rob grinned. ''We'll have a brilliant week,'' he said. ''You'll see. You'll never forget it.''

2

Gerald Matthews tried to decide occasionally why he found Rose Pengelly so attractive. He was a scientist, after all, and trained to be analytical. At first he thought that his loneliness was clouding his judgement. He had few friends of either sex, and after his time alone perhaps he would have been excited by any woman who showed him kindness. But it was more than that. Even before Rose became pregnant, he could tell that other men were fascinated by her. Quite often her house was filled by men, and as she moved among them, pouring wine, laughing, every one of them was affected by her. They become kinder, more vital, more intelligent, because she was there. The sweetest moments for Gerald were when she chose him to be her confidant. She would slip away from the crowd, pull on her jacket, and whisper to him.

"I need some fresh air. Let's leave them to it."

She would tuck her arm into Gerald's, and they would walk down the lane between the overgrown hedges and out onto the rocky path to the headland. The walks over the short grass to the point filled him with joy and hope. For days he would believe that she might come to care for him. Then the magic would wear off, and he would be left with a searing frustration, because nothing ever developed from the friendship. On one of the evenings at Porthkennan he had tried to kiss her. Past the bend in the lane, so they could not be seen from the cottage, he had pulled her clumsily towards him.

With a little laugh she had broken away; then she ran down the lane, leaving a trail of her footprints in the moonlight. At the coast path she turned and called to him, "Come on, Gerald, you old slowcoach," in her old tone, as if nothing had happened. They continued their walk to the headland.

When she told him she was pregnant, he was shattered. He had no idea she had a relationship with anyone else. He thought he was the only man she confided in. When she told him, they were sitting in the kitchen of her cottage. She was perched on the thick windowsill, staring out of the open window down the valley. It was May, and all the trees were in blossom.

"Who is the father?" Gerald demanded. He might have been a Victorian patriarch.

"That's not important," she said, seeming not to realise how upset he was. "Not really. I wanted to be a mother again before it's too late."

It was true that it was almost too late. One of the mysteries of her attraction was that she made no pretence of her age. Her dark hair was streaked at the front with grey, and her hands were rough and lined like an old woman's hands. She had teenage children from a marriage which had finished years before.

Rose Pengelly made her living by letting her converted farm buildings to families in the summer and to birdwatchers in the spring and autumn. The house was usually chaotic, but she seemed not to mind the visitors' wandering in, disturbing her work. She also designed knitwear and had developed a thriving mail order business. She made bright exotic jerseys with motifs of birds and butterflies. Often she wore her own creations, and as she grew larger, she favoured long shapeless cardigans and fringed shawls. She looked like an Indian squaw. Throughout her pregnancy she continued to work. She drove an old blue minivan and took cones of coloured wool and patterns to the women in the neighbourhood who knitted for her. By then it was autumn, and when Gerald came to the house, the strands of wool strung around the kitchen were orange, yellow, and brown. The birdwatchers came as usual, too.

15

She charged them little, and they slept in bunks in the barn. Rose provided breakfast for them, and each morning in October she was in the kitchen by the big white cooker grilling bacon, frying eggs, huge and fertile. Gerald found it hard to stay away.

The baby, a daughter, was born at home on Christmas Eve. Gerald visited the following day, his arms filled with presents for them both. In the kitchen was a decorated tree, and Rose's older children drinking beer with their friends. They seemed to take their mother's confinement for granted and hardly acknowledged him as he walked through on his way to the bedroom. There the baby lay on her back in a wooden cradle, her arms and fingers moving, anemone-like towards the ceiling. Gerald expected Rose to be different, changed by the experience of giving birth, but she was just the same. She was sitting up in bed knitting. Outside it was almost dark, and the room was warm and softly lit. She smiled at him and opened the presents excitedly, so the wrapping was scattered over the big bed and fell onto the floor. The baby was named Matilda.

At first that winter was blissful. There were weeks of clear days with sunshine and cold mornings. Occasionally there was a little frost. There were no birdwatchers in the bunkhouse, and Gerald had Rose to himself. She never mentioned Matilda's father, and he never asked. She seemed to have no contact with him. There were no unexpected visitors at the cottage. Sometimes Gerald dreamed that he might ask Rose to marry him, but he could not bring himself to do it. It was not only the fear of rejection which prevented him from proposing to her. It was the honesty which told him that such a marriage could never work. Rose was so cluttered and untidy. When her older children came home from college, the house was full of their noisy music and loud, confident voices. It was a relief then to go back to his own home, a clean modern house on an estate in Heanor.

Yet still he went back to her, and for a while he was content with her company. As the days grew longer, his mood changed, and the aching depression and frustration returned. He picked quarrels with her and stayed away from the cottage

16

for days. She seemed not to notice his churlishness, though, and when he made an excuse to go to Porthkennan, she greeted him with her usual good temper.

He had moved to Cornwall when he was in his late twenties. He was a graduate in electronics, and before the move he had held a responsible post with a high technology company near Bath. He had come to Cornwall on his way to Scilly, as many birdwatchers did every autumn. The idea of moving there had begun as a romantic fantasy. He dreamed it would solve all his problems but at first did not take the idea seriously. It was true that he hated the tedious and undemanding work of the factory. He hated Wiltshire, too—it was so full of people and so bad for birds. And he hated the people he worked with—or perhaps he envied them their cosy family lives, their friendly games of squash, their girlfriends. It had always been hard for him to keep girlfriends. It was because he was too honest, he told himself. He refused to put on the airs and pretensions of these southerners. These southern women, with their soft ways and their poses, never appreciated honesty. He was a Yorkshireman and proud of it.

It occurred to him on one of his holidays that he could work for himself there. It might be beneath him to mend televisions and washing machines, but he could earn his living. Yet still he was reluctant to leave the security of employment and move to the south-west. It was only when an uncle died and left him some money that he decided quite suddenly to move and to set up in business for himself. The fact that he had taken such a risk still surprised him. When Matilda was born, he had lived in Cornwall for twelve years.

Some of the more open-minded birdwatchers trusted him sufficiently to give him information about rare birds in the country.

Gerald and Rose met through birdwatching. Now, after the baby's birth, he used it as an excuse to go out with her. He would phone her to tell her about rare birds in the southwest, and he, Rose, and Matilda would travel together to see them. He was proud to be seen in their company. It showed that he was not like the other maladjusted lonely birdwatchers who had to go to Thailand or the Philippines to buy them-

17

selves women. It made him like everyone else, a part of a cosy family.

Rose had persuaded him to book for Rob Earl's pelagic trip. "It'll be great," she said. "You'll love it. And it'll be good to have you around here while the party is staying." So then it was impossible for him to refuse.

"I can't spare the time," he said, weakening. "Not a whole week."

"Come just for the boat trip, then."

"Will you come out on the boat with us?" he asked.

But she had laughed and refused to commit herself.

Jane Pym wanted a drink. It had been a long day. In the morning a client who had discharged himself from psychiatric hospital slit his wrists in the waiting room. This was not an unusual occurrence—his hands and face were covered with evidence of self-mutilation—but it made a mess, and there was a new receptionist who overreacted, so the whole day was disrupted, and later interviews were conducted to the background noise of her tears. Jane Pym was forty, an experienced probation officer, but today she felt she was only keeping control of her work by an immense effort of will. There had been other days like that, and they had always ended in disaster.

Perhaps she should plead illness and go home. But Roger would be at home, and she was more disturbed by him than by her clients. She made a large mug of instant black coffee and began to see the people who were waiting for her.

The first client was a young man, a heroin addict who asked to be referred to the drug dependence unit of the hospital which had previously housed the wrist-slitter. Jane listened without sympathy or involvement. She was good at her job, but she had seen too many young addicts. Now they bored her. She no longer believed in their declarations of imminent reform. It was never that easy.

Then there came routine enquiries from the mother of a prisoner who wanted details of the probation coach which carried visitors to the nearest remand centre, and from a young mother whose gas was threatened with disconnection.

18

Jane dealt briskly with the immediate problems and ignored the glances, the hesitation, as her clients went out. They were hoping she would ask: "Is there anything else? How can I help you?" so they could unload onto her the loneliness of their lives, the stories of husbands' infidelity and children's ingratitude. At least Roger and I never had children, she thought, as she hardened her heart and showed them to the door.

Just before lunch one of her favourite customers came in. From her office Jane could hear Mary down the corridor calling cheerfully to the receptionist, who was still sniffing into her handkerchief. Mary was an elderly Irish woman, an alcoholic who had no permanent address and was often seen wandering around one of Bristol's modern shopping centres. She always dressed in layers of clothes, like a Russian grandmother, and in the hot weather, she smelled. She wanted money. She only ever came to see Jane when she wanted money.

"Where are you living now, Mary?" Jane asked. There had to be the pretence of an interview before she handed over the cash. It was a ritual they both understood.

The woman winked. "I've got friends," she said proudly. "I've always got somewhere to stay."

Eventually Jane had given her money. She had a sudden foolish impulse to take Mary out for a meal. She wanted to feel her gratitude and childish happiness in the shared experience. She realised just in time that would have been unprofessional, so Jane just saw her to the door, slipped a few pound coins from her purse into the wrinkled brown hand, and wished her luck.

"Good luck to yourself," the old woman said, "though you'll not be needing it, a fine lady like you!"

And they say that the Irish have second sight! Jane thought.

In the afternoon she left the grimy office on one of the city's bleakest housing estates and drove to a smart village just beyond the suburbs to interview a separated mother before writing a contested custody report for the divorce court. The woman was educated, superficially civilised but more bitter and dishonest than any of Jane's clients from the criminal court. Jane returned with relief to the office. She had more in common with the separated mother than she liked to admit, and the similarity disturbed her. She began to write the report but could not concentrate and knew she would have to complete it while she was in Cornwall.

At five-thirty Jane hovered in the tearoom, hoping that one of her colleagues would suggest that they should go for a drink after work, but everyone else hurried away, and she was forced at last to go home.

She knew as soon as she walked in through the door that Roger was furious. There was a pile of suitcases in the carpeted hall, and he was waiting for her. The house seemed lifeless and empty. Watching his anger, she felt as detached as she had been when interviewing the heroin addict. She could recognise how good-looking he still was despite his grey hair and lined face. She could remember how she had loved him.

"You know I wanted to start early," he fumed. "You promised me you'd be back on time tonight. It'll be midnight before we get to Rose Pengelly's."

"I'm sorry," she said. She *was* sorry. She liked Rose. She liked Cornwall.

He looked at her suspiciously. "You haven't been to the pub with all your friends from the office?"

She roused herself to self-righteous anger, too.

"No," she said. "Of course not. I'm a probation officer, not a teacher. I don't have twelve weeks' holiday and finish work at four o'clock in the afternoon."

"No," he said. "I'm sorry."

She could not tell what he was thinking but knew he was not sorry. He never regretted anything. He was humouring her. He often treated her as one of the difficult adolescent girls he taught at school. She knew he hated teaching the girls. He could shout and rage at the boys or tease them with his sarcastic good humour, but he was afraid of making the girls cry.

"Can we go now?" he asked, trying to restrain his impatience. "Everything's packed. We're all ready."

He's frightened I'll make a scene, she thought, surprised

by his politeness. As she followed him to the car, she felt suddenly and irrationally more hopeful. It would be pleasant to be cut off from the town for a while. Seawatching made Roger happy, and he liked being with other birdwatchers.

He had always been competitive, and it mattered immensely to him that he had seen a greater number of species than any other birder in Britain. He was famous. In every gathering he was surrounded by admiring twitchers, and he relaxed and blossomed. Perhaps there was the chance of a peaceful week, a return to the old closeness. They had spent their honeymoon in Sennen, in a small hotel by the shore. She had been young; marriage had made her feel tranquil, generous. She had thought they would be happy forever. Now she was forty and tired, and she wanted a drink.

Anne James was supervising her daughter's piano practise. She sat on the arm of a chair looking over Lucy's shoulder to the music. Sunshine came into the room from the open French window. Outside in the orchard the fruit was reaching its best. Like Lucy, she found it hard to give her full attention to the playing. She loved summer in Somerset, but she was worried about her husband, and her anxiety had clouded the whole day. He had been working too hard recently, she thought. He had always been too conscientious. She listened for his car on the drive. The news that he had arranged a long weekend away in Cornwall had delighted her. She felt he needed a holiday, and besides, she could savour the last of the summer better without him.

Duncan James heard the piano through the window and saw his wife and daughter from the hall through an open door. He still felt a stranger in this house, though they had been living there for more than a year, partly because it was so much grander than anything he had known as a child and partly because it was, in every way that mattered, Anne's house. He had bought it, but she had created it. She expressed herself through it as other people expressed themselves through work or art. Sometimes he felt she considered him and the children as essential but integral parts of the house, like the crockery or the linen. She tended to them as

21

she tended to the garden. He was not offended by that. He was only glad she was happy.

He stared at his wife and daughter, seeing them as if the drawing room was a stage set and his family characters in a play. It was a light, spacious room. Anne, of course, had chosen the furniture. There was a lot of polished wood. The play, he thought, would be Victorian, rather sentimental.

Anne looked up from the keys, saw him, and smiled, but Lucy was staring at her fingers and did not notice he was there. She was eight, thin and brown, as quick-moving as a fish. It was an effort for her to sit at the piano, and she fidgeted on the stool and swung her legs. Duncan watched her with love, astounded again that he could have produced something so beautiful, glad that he was able to provide for Lucy and Philip a childhood so different from his own. Lucy had her pony, her pretty bedroom, her best friend to stay at weekends. Philip, three years younger, was already more confident than Duncan had ever been. Yet still he could not believe that it would last. He was convinced that in the end he would be left with nothing.

Anne often told him that his insecurity was caused by an inferiority complex, that he deserved his success, but he never believed her. Any of his achievements had been inspired by her. Even now he wondered how she had come to marry him. He had always been ugly, shortsighted, stooped. He still spoke with a heavy west-country accent, and her voice was so light and pretty.

He walked hesitantly into the room, kissed his wife, then stood beside her while Lucy continued to play.

"I'm sorry I have to go away," he whispered over the child's bent head. "Are you really sure you don't mind?"

"Of course not." She smiled. "There's plenty to do here. You need a break."

He thought with bitter amusement how strange it was that she should consider that the week in Cornwall would be a pleasure for him. Perhaps she felt he would be more at ease there. He had been born only twenty miles from Rose Pengelly's cottage, and she had a romantic notion that he needed to return occasionally to his roots.

22

Lucy finished the scale she was playing and looked at her mother in supplication.

"I must have had twenty minutes practise now," she said. "Isn't it time to go out to play?"

Her mother nodded, and Lucy was away, out through the French window towards the end of the orchard, where her brother was playing on a swing.

"Hey!" Anne shouted. "Aren't you going to say goodbye to your father? He'll be away this week."

Lucy stopped in her tracks and came back into the room.

"Is it work?" she said.

"Sort of."

She kissed him and disappeared again.

"I'll miss you all," he said suddenly. "Perhaps I shouldn't go."

But Anne smiled at him with maternal indulgence and drove him past the neat gardens filled with flowers to the station.

As the evening grew darker and the pubs along the harbour wall became rowdy with holidaymakers and Friday-night drinkers, Louis Rosco prepared the *Jessie Ellen* for the next day's charter.

Other boat owners in Heanor paid eager young men to scrub out and stock up with supplies, but Rosco preferred to do the work himself. He had sacrificed too much for the *Jessie Ellen* to entrust her to some lad who skipped school because he thought the sea meant adventure or a fortune from the fishing.

As Rosco carried boxes of beer aboard, he thought with gratitude that birdwatchers did not have such strong stomachs as the divers who usually chartered the boat, and he need not take so much booze. The seawatching trips were a relatively new venture, and he was grateful to Rose Pengelly for having put him onto it. He started to think about Rose Pengelly but stopped himself. It would not do to brood.

When his work was finished, he went to the Blue Anchor for a drink. It was in a side street just up the hill from the harbour, so grimy and unwelcoming that most holidaymakers ignored it, and the locals who patronised it were spared the loud voices, pink thighs, and smell of suntan oil which pervaded the other pubs near the quay. When he went through the door, there was a sudden silence, and he knew they were all looking at him. They still wondered how he had come back to Heanor with a flash boat and no bank loan. Let them wonder, he thought. He ordered a drink and sat alone in a corner with his back to the room. The buzz of conversation resumed.

Louis Rosco had been one of a big family who lived hand-to-mouth in an almost derelict cottage on the shore by Porth-kennan. The mother had been feckless and easy. She'd do anything, they said, for a rum and shrub. Louis remembered her with affection as laughing and generous. His father had been a thin, sickly man, a grafter who took any work that was going—potato picking, casual shifts in the fish factory, and washing dishes in the big hotels in Penzance in the summer. Everyone said he would work himself into the grave, but it was Ellen Rosco who went first. She died quite suddenly in her early forties, when she was walking with a sailor from Falmouth down Harbour Street. She had a massive heart attack and frightened the sailor so much that he almost fell into the water. People talked of nothing else for months.

The family split up then. Most of them were old enough to earn their living, and the others left soon after. Old man Rosco stayed on in the cottage, working in the fish factory until he was old enough to draw a pension, then doing odd gardening jobs in the big houses round Porthkennan. The children scattered all over the country. If anyone asked old man Rosco if he had heard from them or how they were doing, he would vaguely nod but give no details. There had been so many. Perhaps he had lost count and grown confused.

Then Louis had come back with the *Jessie Ellen* and a master's ticket. He was forty-five, thin and small like his father, secretive about his past. Old man Rosco lived only long enough to be taken out for a trip on the *Jessie Ellen* and bought a drink in the Blue Anchor. Louis took over the cottage and put the boat out for charter to divers and fishermen.

He was polite to the people who tried to talk to him, but he gave nothing away. They invented their own explanations for his return. There was something hard about him, they said. He must have been in the army or the navy. He had the look of someone who'd been to prison. Perhaps he had committed some terrible crime.

In the Blue Anchor Louis had one drink, then drove back to Porthkennan. He slowed down past Myrtle Cottage as the road steepened, and he saw the light in the baby's room and the shadow of Rose Pengelly in the kitchen.

3

They met late in the evening on Heanor Quay. Below them the *Jessie Ellen* moved with the incoming tide. They stood in shy groups at first, awkward and uncertain what to do. The boat was in darkness. Then Rob Earl emerged from the nearest pub with a clipboard and a list of names, and Louis Rosco came in his rust-holed van, with Rose and the baby in the passenger seat. She could bring the child, Louis had said. He had nothing against it. He had never yet heard of a baby who had been ill on a boat, and if the others didn't mind, he didn't think she'd get in the way. Then the thin, silent boy who assisted Louis came on a bicycle, and Fat Freddy, who did the cooking, waddled down from the town. Freddy had been sacked from one of the big hotels for erratic timekeeping but said he didn't mind. He preferred going out with the charter boats. It was a better sort of life. Almost immediately there was a smell of coffee.

"I'll need some help with the chum," Rob said. "Louis brought it in the van, but we'll need to get it on board."

"Chum?" Duncan James said. He thought the weekend would be a nightmare. He hated the sea.

Rob looked at him as if he were an idiot. What was he doing on a trip like this if he had never heard of chum?

"It's the bait to bring the seabirds to the boat."

"What's in it?" George asked.

"Fish heads, fish guts, popcorn, and the leftover oil from

the chip shop in Heanor. We hire a cement mixer to mix it. It's in drums in the back of Louis' van."

At last, when the drums were stacked on deck, they were allowed on board. They stood, leaning against the deck rail, looking at the lights of the town.

"We're still missing one," Rob said. "Greg Franks." He looked at his watch. "We'll give him ten minutes; then we'll have to start without him."

George, already mesmerised by the motion of the boat and the dream of new birds, hoped that Greg stayed away. He wanted no distractions. There is nothing, he thought, echoing Rob Earl's words, more exciting than seawatching.

Terry, the thin adolescent, was preparing to cast off when there was the squeal of brakes as a car turned into the harbour carpark, shattering the quiet, robbing George of his dreams. The purple Mercedes had been replaced by a small red sports car. They heard the loud music of its stereo when the engine was turned off, then as soon as that was quiet, Greg Franks' voice. He had lost his Bristol accent. He was rootless, classless. A modern Gypsy, George thought. Or a mercenary. Greg shouted to them that there were some friends in Exeter he had to look up. Business. They knew how it was.

As Terry helped him aboard and the engine started, he was still talking, shouting to be heard, so they missed the exact moment of departure. He hadn't been in the country long, he said. He'd just done India, Pakistan, Nepal. Of course he'd been before, but there was some endemic stuff he still needed. No offence to Rob, of course, but really, travelling alone was the only way to do it. I mean, those group trips. All dudes and wrinklies. He paused and smiled around at them encouraging their agreement.

"I'm not talking about pelagics, of course," he said. "I mean, this is something else. I've been looking forward to this for months." He beamed round at them again and winked. "With the birds I hope to get this weekend," he said, "I hope to extend my list considerably. You never know, I might even get close to Roger's."

Then, without waiting for an answer, he led them into the

saloon and held court to them, mocking and entertaining them, not allowing them to forget him for a moment.

George would have put off delivering the Franks' message to Greg, but Molly would not allow it. He could sense her disapproval across the saloon, and though he tried to ignore it, to concentrate on the field guides and monographs spread over the table, on the characteristics of Madeiran and Wilson's petrels, he knew she was right.

Eventually, feeling pompous and feeling in a superstitious way that what he was doing would bring them bad luck, that by breaking the circle of attention on the seabirds he would spoil their chances of seeing them, he asked if he could talk to Greg on deck.

"Sure," Greg said. "Of course, George."

His tone was still breezy and confident, but George sensed a watchfulness, a challenge, and when the message was passed on, a relief. They stood at the stern of the boat, watching the lights of the mainland disappearing behind them.

"What's this all about?" he said lightly. "Why the mystery?"

"Your parents sent me here to find you," George said.

"Hey! What do you mean? What's wrong? I mean, why the drama?"

"They want to sell your father's business," George said. "They felt you should be consulted. They didn't know how to get in touch with you."

"I've been around," Greg said defensively. "I've been living in Bristol actually. I phone them sometimes."

George shrugged. "That's none of my business," he said. "They hired me to give you a message, and I'm passing it on."

"What exactly is this message, then?"

"They'd like you to go home to discuss the sale of the business." George hesitated, feeling some distaste before continuing, "They say that a share of the profit might be yours."

"Do they, then? Good old Mum and Dad!" Greg grinned. "I'll give them a ring tomorrow night," he said, "as soon

28

as we get back. Tell them you've been a good boy and passed on the message. Put their minds at rest.''

"Yes,'' George said. "That might be kind.''

"How did you know where to find me?'' Greg asked. "Were you booked onto the pelagic anyway?''

"No,'' George said. "A letter from Rob Earl confirming your place on the trip was sent to your parents' home. Your mother opened it.''

Greg swung round suddenly. George hardly recognised him.

"The cow!'' he said. "The lying old cow. She promised she'd never open my letters again.''

But when he got to the saloon, all trace of anger had vanished, and he was the life and soul of the party again.

All night the *Jessie Ellen* moved steadily south-west against an increasing westerly wind. No one slept well. The bunks were hard flat shelves built into the bulkhead, and there were no real mattresses. The cabins were near to the engine, and below deck it was dark, noisy, and very hot. They were crowded and uncomfortable.

George woke when it was still quite dark and Molly was still asleep. The cabin door was open, and Rob was calling him.

"I'm going on deck,'' Rob said softly. "Are you coming?''

"What's the time?''

"Early. It's not properly dawn yet, but I want everything ready before they all get up.''

On deck there was still a fresh wind which blew gusts of spray.

"Where exactly are we?'' George asked.

Rob Earl was in the stern of the boat squatting over a bucket of herring, chopping it roughly on a board. He looked up.

"I hope you're not asking me to give away the secrets of the Wilson's Triangle,'' he said with mock horror. "Every birdwatching club in Britain would start chartering boats to take them. Then how would my company make any profit?''

"I'm hardly likely to set up in competition.''

29

"We've followed the long-liners," Rob said. "They're fishing boats from Spain and northern France which use lines, not trawls. The men gut the fish on the spot, and that attracts the birds. The *Jessie Ellen* has sophisticated radar, so we can follow the other boats. We must be about sixty miles southwest of the Bishop Rock."

The sky was beginning to lighten. George could make out the details of the *Jessie Ellen* and the shapes of the European long-liners in the distance.

Rob turned back to the herring and began to throw it into a wide-meshed canvas bag which already contained pieces of polystyrene float.

"What are you doing?"

"This is the rubby dubby bag," Rob said. "It's brilliant for attracting great shearwater. The bag's dragged along behind the boat and brings the birds in."

He fastened the bag to a fine rope and let it out behind the boat.

By now it was quite light. Louis Rosco came from the saloon, nodded briefly to them, and went into the wheelhouse. Fat Freddy brought them mugs of tea. George could see the fishing boats quite clearly. One of the deckhands on the nearest raised his hand and waved to them. George had the light-headed, empty feeling that comes in the early morning after too little sleep.

I'm like an addict needing a fix, he thought. I won't feel whole and normal until I see a new bird.

Rob said he would go below to wake the others, and soon after, Greg Franks walked unsteadily onto deck. He sat down, his back firmly against the wall of the saloon, the telescope on a tripod between his knees. As he set up the telescope, his hands were shaking, and his face had no colour at all.

"What's the matter?" Rob asked, not really concerned, teasing, knowing the answer already.

"Seasick," said Franks, as if the effort of speech itself provoked nausea.

"Wouldn't you be more comfortable lying down?" George asked.

"I'm not moving anywhere," Greg said, still tight-lipped, "until I've had Wilson's petrel."

And he sat there on the port side grim and silent, his eyes and his attention focused on the sea.

The others drifted onto deck and huddled against the gusting west wind in big coats and jerseys. Most were quiet and pale, suffering from too little sleep and seasickness. Only Roger Pym was loud and healthy, complaining because Jane had been ill in the night and kept him up, and irritating them by his demands for breakfast. They crowded at the stern of the boat watching the rubby dubby bag bouncing over the waves scattering shreds of herring behind it.

As the first rays of the sun broke through the thin cloud, a group of petrels began to follow the boat, attracted by the fish. They were storm petrels, common in Britain, but reassuring. Anything now seemed possible.

"Wilson's petrel!"

The sound burst from Greg Franks and was so loud and joyful that no one realised at first who had shouted. Molly had been concerned because he seemed so ill. She still felt that they were responsible for him and should deliver him back to his mother safe and intact. Now his recovery seemed miraculous. He was standing at the deck rail pointing out the bird to the others, his face flushed with excitement. To Molly the bird seemed indistinguishable from the storm petrels which were still following the boat, but the others were convinced by the identification. Look at the size! they said. Look at the length of the leg! The bird circled the boat, then pattered behind it with the storm petrels before flying away.

With the arrival of the bird there was an immediate release of tension. This was what they had paid a fortune for and travelled to Cornwall to see. Only Rob Earl and Roger Pym had seen Wilson's petrel before; the others felt the aquisitive euphoria of a new bird. They gathered around Greg.

"What a brilliant piece of identification!" George said. "How could you tell at that distance that the bird was a Wilson's?"

"Well," Greg said, "once I'd got my eye in, it wasn't that difficult."

31

The others joined in the congratulations, but Molly, standing as always apart and observant, thought they were disappointed it was Greg who had found the bird. They would have preferred it to be someone else.

"I'm going to lie down now," Greg said. "I still don't feel well."

"Where will you be?" Rob asked. "In case we need to call you. In your cabin?"

"No, it's too stuffy below. I'll just crash out on deck. Don't call me unless it's a tick."

"We won't know whether or not it's a tick," Roger Pym said quickly. "We haven't seen your list."

"It won't be a tick," Greg said grandly, "unless it's a first for Britain."

He walked slowly towards the bow and curled up out of sight in the sun.

Those who were feeling strong enough had a celebratory breakfast in the saloon. They ate piles of scrambled eggs, drank milky coffee, and listened to Rob Earl and Roger Pym argue the finer points of Wilson's petrel field identification. Someone opened a bottle of whisky.

Then everyone wandered back onto deck. George was enjoying himself more than he had done for years. The sun was high above the horizon and warmer. The cloud had disappeared and the wind had dropped. There was a smell of salt and fish, wet rope, and diesel. The *Jessie Ellen* was moving in a large circle around the long-liners. They saw more petrels and two great shearwaters skimming and turning over the waves. In all his years of seawatching he had known nothing like it. He was relaxed and exhilarated. The sunlight had tightened the skin on his face, so he felt younger. The deck where he sat was comfortably warm. The others were sitting at the stern watching the rubby dubby bag, but he wanted to be alone and sat where Greg Franks had been, his back against the saloon, his legs straight ahead of him. Rob had once described seawatching as a cross between meditation and therapy. George thought about it and laughed. It had been right to come.

He focused his binoculars at random farther away from

the boat towards the horizon and saw a bird which he knew immediately he had never seen before. It was a petrel, dark-rumped. At first he thought it might be Leach's, but the tail was the wrong shape. As it turned and wheeled against the reflected sunlight, there was a flash of white on the wings.

He did not want to make a fool of himself. The light and the lack of sleep might be deceiving. It was hard to use a telescope on the moving boat, but he set it up and looked at the bird again through it. He forced himself to concentrate. Perhaps Rob Earl sensed his sudden tension, because he stood up and moved along the deck rail towards George.

"What have you got?" he asked softly.

"I haven't a clue," George said. "Really. A dark-rumped petrel. Not Leach's. Not big enough. There's a white flash on the wing. And huge feet. Enormous red-webbed feet."

Rob set up his own telescope and looked with a passionate concentration, then swore under his breath.

"It's a long way off now," he said. "But you're right about the feet. They're bloody enormous. Even from here."

When Rob called to Louis Rosco to manoeuvre the *Jessie Ellen* nearer to the bird, there was such an edge of urgency in his voice that he alerted the others, and the peace of the day was shattered. The tone of the engine changed. The people at the stern were shouting to know what had been seen. There was noise, confusion, and excitement.

"We'll have to attract the bird closer with the chum," Rob shouted. He tried to pull the bin of fish oil and offal towards the side, but it was too heavy, and he could not get a grip on it. His feet were slipping on the wet floor.

"Get off your backsides and help me, someone!" he shouted, frustration turning to anger. "Can you still see it, George? Don't bloody lose it."

Gerald Matthews tried to life the bin from behind, and the stinking oil slopped over the side onto their clothes. Rob took no notice and continued shouting instructions to Louis.

They levered the bin so it was balanced on the deck rail.

"Wait!" he said. "We need to put out the chum so the wind blows it towards the bird."

Then at last they tipped the contents overboard. The oily

33

film spread over the water, mixed with popcorn and pieces of fish. It moved slowly but eventually covered a far greater area than George would have thought possible. The boat began to chug away from it.

"Where are we going?" Roger Pym yelled in panic. "We need that bird."

He was nowhere to be seen when Rob needed help with the chum. Now he was right on the deck rail seeking the best possible view of the petrel.

"We'll turn back soon," Rob said, "and circle the area of chum. Louis knows what he's doing. We've used this technique before."

"Four Wilson's petrels!" Gerald Matthews shouted. But now their attention was focused on the new bird and they hardly turned to look, and when Rose Pengelly lifted Matilda high in the air to look at the string of shearwaters, they looked at her angrily because she was distracting them.

Impassively Louis Rosco turned the *Jessie Ellen*, and it began slowly to circle the area of chum. Rob had disappeared into the saloon and returned with field guides, photographic guides. He and George pored over them, becoming more impatient and excited, as they could find nothing which fitted the description of the bird they had seen.

"Are you sure it wasn't Leach's or Wilson's?" Roger Pym said at last. He sounded irritated and petulant.

"Oh, yes." George said firmly. "Quite sure."

"Matsudeira's? Tristram's?"

"No. There were the feet, you see. Quite startling."

Then they began to consider the possibility that it was a bird as yet unrecorded, a species like that recently discovered breeding in a small colony on the Salvage Islands. It would be impossible to have such a record accepted on only a fleeting view, and they peered over the rail at the oily water, tense and silent. The air and the water were filled with birds but no one could make out the red-footed petrel.

"There it is!" Rob said triumphantly. "Just there. Under the crowd of gulls. Look at that head and that underwing! Pass me the camera. We'll need photographs. If I had a gun, I'd shoot the bloody thing."

Then, obliging, showing off almost, it circled above them, so they could see the brilliant red feet and the light shining through the shafts of the wing feathers. It was possible to detail the wing, to draw the pattern of each feather. They drank in the image of the bird, sketching it, memorising the joy of the moment. George felt drawn to it. It was the climax of sixty years of birdwatching. No other experience would match it. He could not take his eyes off the bird.

He heard Jane Pym ask hesitantly if she should go to fetch Greg, and for a moment he felt guilty because he had given the boy no thought.

"I'll go," Duncan James said. "This is very interesting, but I'm afraid its rather above me."

George wondered that anyone could be so unmoved by the beauty of the bird, by the excitement of discovery, and heard the man move clumsily away.

The bird flew back to feed on the chum, and the boat continued to circle it. As the *Jessie Ellen* moved slowly through the water, they saw the petrel in different lights from different angles. Rob took photograph after photograph.

"It's quite different from anything else I've ever seen," George said. "Really, I don't think there can be any mistake."

At last they were able to relax. They felt they knew the bird and would always remember it. It was almost as if they owned it. Rob put down the camera, lay back on the deck, and stretched.

"Where's Greg?" he asked. "If he doesn't get here soon, he'll miss it." Without moving from his place in the sun, he turned his head and shouted. "Duncan! Where's Greg?"

The older man walked back along the deck towards them. He seemed helpless, rather ashamed, like a child who has failed to perform a simple task.

"I'm sorry," he said. "I can't find him. You'll have to help."

"What do you mean, you can't find him?" Rob was beyond himself after the new bird, superior, derisive.

"He's not on deck where he went to sleep," Duncan said, "and he's not in his bunk. I don't know where else to look."

"He'll be here somewhere," Rob said at his most irritatingly flippant. "On the last trip I did, Keith Vinicombe fell asleep in a lifeboat, and we thought we'd lost him overboard."

He stretched again.

Molly and George helped Duncan James to look for Greg. At first it was a chore, and they thought it would soon be over. They searched the boat from end to end, growing more bewildered and disturbed as they failed to find any sign of Greg Franks. It was as if he had never existed. His clothes, his bag, his binoculars, and the telescope had all disappeared. As he was rooting fruitlessly through a storage space in the bulkhead, George remembered suddenly a nightmare which had recurred when his first son was a baby. He dreamed he had taken the boy in his pram into a strange and busy town, then left him on a street corner and forgotten about him. Later, when he returned in panic to look for the pram, all sign of it and the baby had gone, and he ran helplessly round the streets in a futile search. The search for Greg Franks had the same nightmare quality. Finally they called the others to help them, and they chased round the boat in a frenzy, calling Greg's name, angry because they felt he must be playing some elaborate practical joke.

Rose Pengelly found Greg, and she had stopped looking for him. Throughout the search she was calmer than the others. She searched the cabins carefully but without their panic. Then Matilda, who had been sleeping in a carrycot in the saloon, woke up, and Rose said she would have to attend to her. She would need changing. She would be hungry. She took the baby to the deck at the stern of the boat. It was midafternoon, and that was the only part of the boat still in sunlight. Louis was already steering the boat back towards land. She put a rug on the deck and sat there, feeding the baby, quite content it seemed, despite the disappearance of the young man, quite self-contained.

When she screamed, Louis got to her first. He could not tell what was wrong with her. Her mouth was open with horror, but she could not speak. He could see nothing out of order. The baby was still feeding with muffled murmurs of

36

delight. The rubby dubby bag, now almost empty, still attracted a stream of petrels and gulls.

Rose pointed to the rubby dubby bag.

"Look," she said at last.

Louis reluctantly left her. By now the others were coming from below in response to her scream. He stood at the stern rail and looked down at the bag. Something had become entangled with the rope, and as the floating bag bounced over the waves, so did the piece of flotsam. He saw a shoe first. The foot apparently was caught in the rope. The rest of the body sank at times under the water, then arched out of it as the *Jessie Ellen* moved over a wave. This was what had made Rose scream.

Louis shouted tersely to the boy to cut the engine and began to pull on the rope which attached the rubby dubby bag to the stern rail. He had to pull gently. Any jerking might disentangle the shoe and send the body back into the water. When it was almost to the level of the deck, he paused to take a breath but would not let the others help him. He motioned them away. It was only when Greg was within reach that he called to them. Then they tried to haul him aboard by hand. The skin was wet and slippery, and they were worried that the clothes might tear or come off. At last they got him onto the deck. Louis turned him over and pumped his back. Water trickled from his mouth. Then Louis tried mouth to mouth resuscitation.

Molly, helpless and incompetent, saw the attempt to revive the boy as a tasteless performance. Louis must have known from the beginning that it would fail. Perhaps he thought the others would be even more disturbed by the young man's death if he did not try.

George was horrified that he was reminded once again of the day at Holywell Pond. The seawater had smoothed the black hair around Greg's face, so he looked again like an animal, a stoat, and on his face there was the same smile of defiant victory.

4

Inspector Claire Bingham lived in a smart new housing estate on the hill outside Heanor. When the National Trust sold the land to meet local housing need, they had not envisaged the split-level bungalows with balconies overlooking the harbour which were finally built there, and the estate caused the Trust considerable embarrassment. The Binghams settled easily into their home. They gave dinner parties for the other professional couples who lived on the hill. They had two cars and changed the largest every year. When work allowed, Claire changed into a pink-striped leotard and jogged and stretched with her neighbours at the aerobics class in the primary school hall. Afterwards she drank coffee with them and discussed mortgage rates and house prices and the problems of being a working mother.

On the weekend of the *Jessie Ellen* trip Claire Bingham was not officially on duty. She spent Saturday morning shopping, pushing Thomas in his buggy strung with carrier bags around a Heanor clogged with holidaymakers. She had expected, when she was pregnant, that Richard would do more of that sort of thing. It seemed so obvious that they had never discussed it. They were both working full-time, weren't they? She earned as much as he did, probably more, especially as his colleagues seemed to pass on all the legal aid work to him these days. He knew she was ambitious, the first detective inspector to return to work after maternity leave in the Devon and Cornwall force. She had expected more of him.

But he was as busy as she was and always seemed to bring work home. Then he pleaded domestic ignorance and incompetence.

"You do all that household stuff better than me," he always said. "If you're tired, don't bother cooking. I'll fetch a takeaway."

It infuriated her that two intelligent people found it impossible to organise their lives more efficiently.

When she received the telephone call on Saturday night asking her to wait on the quay for the *Jessie Ellen*, she knew that she was second choice. She always was. The other duty inspector in her division had thought nothing would come of the emergency call and had suggested that the police station should try her.

"It'll only be an accident," he said. "Some drunken holidaymaker losing his footing and slipping into the water. Claire Bingham's keen. Let her see to it. If she's so bloody efficient about paperwork, let her fill in the forms."

She knew her male colleague would have been contacted first when the coastguard informed the police station about the death at sea. He was approaching retirement and had begun to take things easy. He was always passing routine work on to her.

"I'm just a policeman after all," he would say maliciously but without bitterness. "Not a graduate with a law degree. No accelerated promotion for me."

She felt sometimes that the law degree, which in the beginning had seemed so valuable, was a disadvantage. So was her accent—BBC English, with a trace of Sloane Ranger learned at public school—and the fact that her husband was a defence solicitor. Her friends from school and university thought she was mad to have joined the force. The liberals among them saw the police as state-sponsored thugs, and the snobs considered policemen to be working class morons with dirty fingernails. Only Richard, doubtful at first, had stuck by her. Now she never told chance aquaintances what work she did.

It would have been impossible for her to explain to them that from the moment of joining the police she had felt com-

39

pletely at home. She was comfortable with the philosophy of service and discipline, and without the structure she would have felt insecure.

Disapproving college friends who watched her progress from a distance blamed it all on her background. Her father had been an army officer, and before being sent away to school, she had followed him on different postings around the world. She's scared of the real world, they said. She can't cope without authority. They did not know that Claire's mother had been killed by an IRA car bomb in the small town in Germany where her father was based, and that from that day Claire had seized on order, routine, and organisation as her only means of survival.

The administrators within her station thought Claire Bingham was a brilliant officer. She was logical and tidy. She left nothing to chance. Her immediate superiors were more cautious, but they were afraid of being considered prejudiced because she was a woman. They had been told that she had a first-class mind, that she represented the future, and that caused resentment. She was too rigid, they said among themselves. She played it too much by the book. You had to be willing to take risks. She was too defensive.

In these conversations one wise chief inspector said to give her time. She was still young, still inexperienced. She lacked confidence. She might make a good detective yet.

Claire Bingham had no idea why the *Jessie Ellen* had been to sea. She had been told that it was a charter boat, and she expected the passengers to be young men out for a day's fishing, members perhaps of some club. The disparate group which emerged from the saloon as the boat moved slowly towards the quayside shocked her. She watched a thin boy make the boat fast, then waited for them to come ashore. The first person onto the quay was Rose Pengelly. She looked exhausted, and her face was grimy and tearstained. She clutched Matilda in her arms. Claire was horrified by the irresponsibility of taking a baby to sea. What sort of woman, she thought, would expose her child to such danger?

Then she saw the Pyms, a middle-aged couple who were respectably dressed and obviously distressed by the accident,

40

and a tall, upright gentleman with a wife who seemed to have chosen her clothes in a jumble sale. Only then came three single men who might have been fishermen, except for the cameras and telescopes which were draped around their bodies. It was quite different from what she had imagined, and she was thrown by it. For a moment she did not quite know where to begin. It was a new experience for her. The passengers stood on the pier in a miserable group, looking for guidance.

She pulled herself together and approached them. Sergeant Berry took the doctor onto the boat to look at the body.

"I'm Inspector Bingham," she said formally. "South-West Cornwall C.I.D.; I'll need to take statements from you all later."

The spare elderly man detached himself from the group. His voice was polite, but it would be hard to disagree with him. Claire knew immediately that there was something familiar about him. She had seen him before.

"I wonder if we might go home to wait for you," he said. "We're all staying at the same place, with Rose Pengelly at Myrtle Cottage. It's in Porthkennan. Perhaps you could come there to take your statements. As you can imagine, its been a very distressing day."

"Yes," she said. "I think that might be possible, Mr.—?"

"Palmer-Jones," he said. "George Palmer-Jones."

Then she knew where she had seen him. He had been a guest lecturer at Hendon. When the others trooped miserably towards their cars, she called him back.

"Mr. Palmer-Jones," she said. "I just wanted to say what a pleasure it is to meet you again. You were rather a hero of mine at college actually. I read your report of the patrolling of sensitive areas even before I joined the force. At Hendon they told us you were the only civil servant really to understand what policing is about."

She paused, blushing, realising that she was being too effusive, unprofessional.

"I'm sorry," she said. "I'm keeping you from your

friends. I expect I'll see you later. The formalities won't take long if it was an accident.''

He looked up with disturbed, rather angry eyes. He hardly seemed to see her. She was hurt. She had hoped he would take more notice of her.

''I shouldn't be too certain,'' he said, ''that it was an accident.''

He walked back towards his wife, then returned briefly to tell her that Greg's car was still parked on the quayside.

Along the harbour wall, as if from nowhere, a group of people had gathered. The news of the young man's death must be public knowledge already. She turned her back to them and stepped carefully onto the boat. On the deck the doctor was looking at the body with a strong spotlight.

''We might as well move him,'' he said. ''They pulled him around quite a lot trying to revive him.''

''Anything unusual?'' She stooped beside him. There was a strong and unpleasant smell of fish which made her feel sick.

''Only this.'' He seemed to be talking almost to himself. ''A severe blow to the back of the head. It must have knocked him out before he hit the water. That's probably why he drowned so quickly. The water was warm. If he was a swimmer, he could have survived for ages. But I can't see where he can have fallen and hit his head. The deck rail's too low, and if he slipped backwards onto the deck, he wouldn't have fallen into the water. The wound's in the wrong place and the wrong shape for that anyway.''

''What would you say, then?''

He straightened slowly. ''It sounds ridiculous,'' he said, ''but it's the right shape for the classic blunt instrument.''

''Murder?'' she said. ''Are you sure?'' Again it was so far from what she had expected when she came to the quay that she could hardly believe it.

''Well, I don't see how it can have been an accident, and it can't be suicide. He's hardly going to hit himself on the back of the head.''

She stood up, her head spinning with the smell of fish and the exhilaration and awesome responsibility of a murder investigation. It was her case, she thought. They could not take it away from her now. She gripped the deck rail and tried desperately not to be sick.

"Are you all right?"

It was the doctor, thinking the idea of such violence was making her ill. She could have told him that she had come to terms with it years ago.

"Yes," she said. "Fine."

She looked around her and caught the eye of Louis Rosco, who was still standing in the lighted wheelhouse. She nodded towards the body.

"Can you sort this out with my sergeant?" she said. "I want to talk to the skipper and find out what all those people were doing on the boat anyway."

"Birds!" the doctor said.

"What do you mean?" She looked at him suspiciously.

"That's what they were doing on the *Jessie Ellen*. They're birdwatchers. I'm one myself. I went on the same ship three weeks ago. They got me Wilson's petrel."

With that he left her alone on deck and went to talk to Sergeant Berry. Probably, she thought, about women's weak stomachs. The pubs beyond the harbour wall were closing. There were good-humoured calls, the occasional snatch of singing. The crowd peering down at the *Jessie Ellen* was growing.

Louis Rosco watched the policewoman on the deck with a mounting despair and confusion. He had thought these formalities would soon be over. Greg's death would be put down as an accident, and there would be no more questions. Now the sight of the woman bending over the body, talking earnestly to the doctor, made him realise that this hope was quite unrealistic. She was the sort to be curious. She would want to know everything. Even the shape of her depressed him. She was angular and tall, with a sharp nose and pointed chin. Her pale hair was tied away from her face. He sensed that she was well dressed and that some men might find her attractive, but he only had an impression of order and dogged persistence. She frightened him.

43

When she came to the wheelhouse door, Rosco still had no idea what he would tell her.

"Would you like some tea?" he asked. The boy and Fat Freddy had been allowed home after a brief discussion with Sergeant Berry. "I was going to make some anyway. If you've got questions to ask, we'll be more comfortable in the saloon."

She nodded gratefully, and he felt relieved. He showed her where to go, forcing himself to be natural and polite. But as he went to the galley to make the tea, he felt his heart racing and his breath coming unevenly in gulps.

When he returned to the saloon, her legs were crossed, and she rested a notebook on one knee. He handed her a mug and sat on the opposite side of the table on the bench seat.

"Was the dead man a birdwatcher?" she asked. Rosco nodded.

"They all were," he said. "As far as I know. I never realised until I started this business what fanatics they are."

"What do you mean?"

"Well, that they'd go to such lengths to see a few gulls and petrels. It's not cheap to charter the boat for twenty-four hours, an there's the tour company's commission on top of that."

He felt on safe ground and was beginning to relax.

"Where does Mrs. Pengelly come into it?" She remembered the untidy woman with the baby and could not keep the disapproval from her voice.

Panic made it hard for him to think rationally. She was waiting for an answer, and he forced himself to speak.

"She runs a sort of guest house," he said. "Down at Porthkennan at the top of the valley. She has a lot of birdwatchers to stay in the spring and the autumn. After the boat trip the passengers have a few days there. It's all organised by the company in Bristol. A package, like. The Cornish Spectacular they call it. They do four over the summer. This would be the last."

He thought he was speaking too much, but she seemed not to notice his nervousness.

"Was one of the company's representatives on the boat?"

"Yes. Mr. Earl. He's been on every trip. He looks after the birdwatching side of it."

"So he'd have a list of all the passengers?"

"Sure to."

"And he's staying at Porthkennan, too?"

He nodded.

"Was there anything unusual about this trip?" she asked. "Did you notice anything different from the other three?"

He considered.

"They were more serious," he said. "About the birdwatching, like. On the other trips there were one or two fanatics, but most were there to have a good time. They wanted to see the birds, but if they didn't, it wouldn't be the end of the world. On this one you felt it was a matter, well, of life and death."

"Did they see what they wanted to?"

"Yes," he said. "They got themselves into a right state, too. It started off like all the others. They saw Wilson's petrels. That's what they all came out to see. Then there was something else which really excited them. They couldn't identify it; Mr. Earl said it must be something really rare. Perhaps it had never been seen before. That's when we realised the boy was missing. They went to fetch him to show him the new bird, but they couldn't find him."

"He wasn't birdwatching with the others?"

"No," Rosco said. "He'd been seasick in the night and still didn't look well in the morning. He dragged himself out for a couple of hours, then went to lie down again."

"In his bunk?"

"No," Rosco said shortly. "On deck. Mostly they were birdwatching from the stern. He was up this end, where it was a bit quieter."

"Couldn't you see him from the wheelhouse, then?"

"Not directly, no. He was hidden by the saloon."

"But you would have noticed someone going up to him and talking to him?"

Again the panic returned.

"No. You don't know what it was like when they saw that

45

bird. It was pandemonium. They were all shouting and running about. I wasn't thinking about anything else but getting the boat exactly where they wanted her to be.''

Claire found the scene hard to imagine. In her experience adult birdwatchers were elderly, rather dotty women, who fed blue tits in their gardens and went for nature rambles. Most she had met were children—earnest and pretentious schoolboys. The variety described by Rosco seemed implausible. He sensed her incredulity.

"You talk to them," he said. "You'll find out then what they're like.''

She nodded reassuringly. She did not want to offend Louis Rosco. If Franks had been murdered, surely the skipper was the least likely to have anything to do with it. What would a Cornish boatman have to do with a young man from Bristol?

"There was nothing else unusual?" she asked. "No arguments or disagreements?''

"Not exactly," he said. "Not a real row. You had the feeling they were getting at each other, winding each other up, but Friday night was like that on each of the trips. They were worried, Rob Earl said, that they wouldn't see any birds. It seemed to get on their nerves. Then there was all that fuss about lists.''

"Lists?" She was mystified. Perhaps it was some obscure nautical term.

"They all make a list of the birds they've seen. They all wanted the boy that died to tell them the number of his, but he was teasing them, leading them on. 'You'll have to wait and see' he said. 'I'll add it up and let you know tomorrow.' ''

"It sounds very childish," she said.

He shrugged. "You should see some of the fishing parties," he said. He had an irrational desire to defend the birdwatchers. Perhaps it had something to do with Rose Pengelly.

Claire Bingham was starting to feel impatient. She should be at Porthkennan while the other passengers were still tired and shocked. She should not give them too much time to discuss things and concoct a story among them. It was reassuring that George Palmer-Jones was with them. He would give her reliable inside information. But in a way, too, his presence only increased the pressure on her. She did not want to let herself down in front of someone so respected in the profession, someone who could possibly influence her career if he chose. Outside on the deck she heard the voices of the men who were taking away the body. It must have slipped because there was a thud and a muffled oath.

"Are there any more parties booked onto the boat?" she asked.

"Not this week."

"You do realise we'll want to examine it in more detail? There'll be experts to see it first thing in the morning, and there'll be someone here all night."

"Why all this, then?" he asked suddenly. "Don't you think it was an accident?"

"No," she said calmly. "He was hit on the head before he drowned."

"Couldn't he have done that when he fell?"

"Not according to the doctor." She looked at him sharply. "You don't seem very surprised."

He spoke slowly, his hands gripped tightly around his knee.

"When they were looking for him, they couldn't find any of his gear." he said. "Even his bag and the bits of clothes he'd left below had gone. That seemed very queer to me."

"I see," she said, and scribbled something in her note-book.

Rosco stood up. He felt drained and worn out and could no longer think clearly. "Is that all?" he asked.

She nodded. "For now."

"Are you going to Porthkennan?"

"Probably." She had already moved from the saloon and onto the deck. There was a faint breeze, but the air was still hot and humid.

"I live there, too," he said. "I'm in the cottage on the shore. If you want me, that's where I'll be."

He suddenly wanted to prolong the interview. The extent of his folly struck him and cut through his panic. He should have told her. She was sure to find out for herself. Perhaps

47

she already knew but was saying nothing in the hope of catching him out.

"Goodbye, Mr. Rosco," she said formally, and jumped without his help from the boat onto the quay. "I'll probably be talking to you again tomorrow."

He stood for a moment in the doorway of the saloon, unable to move. With the removal of the body the crowd at the harbour wall had faded away. The town was quiet. Her shadow was already disappearing among the cranes, the boxes of cargo, and fish crates on the quay. A uniformed police constable watched her go.

Louis suddenly came to life. He jumped from the *Jessie Ellen* onto the quay.

"Inspector!" he shouted, running after her. "Inspector, there's something I should tell you!" But by the time he reached the constable, Claire Bingham was driving away in her expensive car.

"What's the matter?" the policeman asked. "Can I help you?"

"No," Louis said. "It's nothing that won't wait." He turned to the policeman, who was young, only a boy. "You might as well come aboard," he said. "You'll be more comfortable there. You'll have a long night." Then, because the *Jessie Ellen* provided the only security he had, he added, "I'll stay here with you."

Claire Bingham went first to the police station. Berry had collected Greg Franks' car, and she had arranged to meet him there. Before she did anything, she phoned her husband. She could never quite lose herself in her work. Whatever she was doing, her responsibility for him and for Thomas remained at the back of her mind, a guilty irritation.

"I'm sorry," she said. "I'll be very late."

As she had expected he was bad-tempered.

"What about the morning?" he said petulantly. "What shall I do if you're not back? It's happened before. Who takes Tom to the childminder?"

"You'll have to do it. You know where she lives."

"Claire," he said accusingly, as if she was being awkward

48

deliberately, just to annoy him, "You know I'd arranged early squash with Charlie tomorrow."

She wanted to say that there were lots of things she had arranged, too, and anyway, wasn't murder slightly more important than showing off on the squash court in front of Charlie Turner, but she hated spending time away from him with disagreement lingering between them.

"I'm sorry, darling," she said. "Really sorry. I'll be home as soon as I can."

Sergeant Berry had been in the canteen. She could smell the fried food and stale cigarette smoke around him as he came into the office, though she knew he never smoked. She stood up and opened a window, but away from the sea the night was still, and it did no good. Berry was young, quiet, anonymous. He still lived with his parents in one of the genteel, slightly shabby suburbs of the town. To his colleagues he was something of a joke. He was a nondrinker and had, it seemed, no girlfriends. They knew very little about him.

Claire had come to admire and rather to like him. He was a member of one of the small exclusive eccentric churches which flourish still in the west country, and there *was* a girlfriend she found out, one of the diminishing congregation. She was surprised, too, to discover that Berry had a sharp, unmalicious sense of the ridiculous, and occasionally he had her in fits of giggles, like a schoolgirl.

She sensed he disapproved of her domestic arrangements. She could tell he really thought she should be at home with her son. Yet he never preached. Sometimes his calm patience made her feel inadequate, and then she would lash out at him.

"Do you want to be a dogsbody for the *whole* of your life, Berry?" she would demand. "Don't you want to *live* a bit, experience something more exciting than tea with Mummy and Daddy?"

But she could never provoke him into a reaction. He would shake his head and smile, then melt unobtrusively away.

"Well," she said now, "have you found out anything useful, before we go to Porthkennan?"

"A few things from the computer," he said, so she was immediately excited. He was a master of understatement.

"Anything on Franks?"

"He's never been convicted," Berry said. "He was charged with burglary five years ago when he was still a juvenile but found not guilty."

"Anything else?"

Berry paused, and if it had been anyone else, she would have thought he was doing it to intensify the drama of his revelation.

"Louis Rosco," he said.

"Has he got a record?" she asked. She was disappointed. She expected it to be something trivial. He nodded.

"Arson," he said. "And manslaughter. He got ten years."

"How long's he been out?"

"Four years."

"Any details?"

"Not much. The offence happened in Bristol, and I've been trying to get more information from there. It was a small boat yard. Rosco was working there. They assume it was a grievance against his employer. A security guard was killed."

She was astonished. She would never have thought Rosco capable of such violence. He seemed such an ordinary nondescript sort of man. She was surprised by her own lack of judgement.

She stood up. A nervous energy had kept her going all evening, but now she felt very tired. Perhaps it would be a mistake to do much more tonight, she thought. She should be alert when she was taking the detailed statements. All the same, they would have to go to Porthkennan. By now one of them might be ready to confess. Most murders were cleared up within hours, and the police were given little to do.

Berry was looking at her with a suppressed excitement.

"There is something else," he said.

"What?" Her head was swimming, and she felt she could take in little else.

"I found this in Franks' car. It was in the dashboard. No attempt had been made to hide it."

He held up a polythene envelope of white powder.

"What is it?" she said foolishly.

"We'll need Forensic to test it," he said, "but it looks like heroin."

5

M_{ost} of the trippers who explored the narrow road signposted to Porthkennan were disappointed and turned back before they reached Myrtle Cottage. At first there was little to see. Grey, sheep-cropped moorland rose away from the seaward side of the road, so there were no views of cliffs or water, and the colour of the hillside made it seem always to be in shadow. The monotony of the landscape was broken by granite outcrops, huge and brooding against the sky. After a mile there was a turn in the road and then a row of derelict cottages, windowless, with holes in the roofs and the distinctive chimneys of a disused tin mine. The scene of industrial decay so close to the road had nothing in common with the picture-postcard Cornwall of thatched cottages and cream teas. The trippers thought they had reached Porthkennan and turned back to the main road with relief.

But beyond the abandoned hamlet the lane turned again towards the sea. Like a green scar in the bare hillside, a valley cut through the granite to the coast. Porthkennan was the name of the valley and the scattering of houses which had been built in its shelter. There was no real village, no pub, but a forest of vegetation—trees, shrubs, and large exotic flowers—which seemed to overwhelm the houses. Even in winter the place was lush and green. In the valley the light and heat seemed trapped and intensified. If it had been daytime, Claire Bingham would have seen the whitewashed walls

52

of the houses, dark green leaves, shining blackberries, over-blown roses, all with a startling clarity. Even now, in the car, they were aware of the stillness and the trees all around them. It was like driving into the jungle.

The vegetation was richest near the stream which followed the valley to a small cove. There the water trickled through smooth boulders as big as a child, and across shingle and sand to the waves.

Louis Rosco's cottage was almost on the beach, as lifeless from the outside as one of the miners' cottages on the moor. It had no main electricity, and the water was collected from the roof in a tank. The fishermen in Heanor wondered how he could bear to live there.

Rose Pengelly's place was much grander. Myrtle Cottage was near the head of the valley. Once a small farmhouse and two cottages had stood on the site, but the house had been converted by a previous owner. It was long, predominantly single-storeyed. It faced the sea. Behind it the stream flowed through the garden, and by its side was the barn which Rose had turned into hostel accommodation for birdwatchers.

They waited for the police in the living room in a state of numb exhaustion. Rose made coffee for them, but Rob Earl produced a bottle of whisky, and they drank that instead. When they did speak, it was not about Greg Franks but about the new bird. Molly was unsure whether this burst of excited conversation was a way of avoiding the subject of Greg's death, or whether they were so obsessed with the petrel that nothing else, not even murder, was so important. Roger wanted to begin investigations into the identification of the petrel immediately. The person to contact was Jauanin in Paris, he said. He'd done all that magnificent work on Leach's petrel. If there were any stray unconfirmed records of a large red-footed petrel, he'd know about it. They had to persuade Pym that it might be inconsiderate to telephone so late at night, but still he continued with his plans. They'd have to check all the museums, he said. Many of them, he knew, had piles of unidentified skins, collected by Victorian natu-ralists. It would take a long time, but they would have to check them all. And then, he said, when all the research was done and they were quite sure, they would have to think of a name for the bird.

When Claire Bingham and Berry arrived at the cottage, it was midnight. There was the sharp smell of elderberry. They could hear the shallow running water of the stream behind the house. There was still no moon. Claire knocked at the door gently, remembering that there was a baby in the house, knowing that there is nothing more annoying than to have coaxed a child to sleep only to have it wakened by a thoughtless visitor. It was opened by the dark woman, the mother of the child.

"Mrs. Pengelly?" Claire asked, and Rose motioned her into the living room, where they were all sitting. The inspector saw then that her instinct had been wrong, and she would get little out of them that night. The animation that had inspired the discussion about the petrel had faded. They were blank and listless. Some of them had been drinking. There was a bottle of whisky on a small table and empty glasses on windowsills, chair arms, the floor. There was, it seemed, little grief. Rather she felt a communal and overwhelming tiredness. She asked them to introduce themselves, and as they gave their names, she thought how ordinary and respectable they seemed.

"Can anyone tell me how Greg Franks died?" Claire Bingham asked. She spoke a little too loudly, fighting against tiredness. "Someone must have seen something."

They looked at her in silent and unresponsive hostility. So much for a confession, she thought, and an early end to the case.

"Look," she said. "I don't think there's a lot of point in taking detailed statements tonight. If anyone has any information about Mr. Franks, you should tell me now. But it's late, and you must tired, and if you really think you can't help, I've no objection to most of you going to bed. I'll leave Sergeant Berry here to look after you."

"Make sure we don't run away, do you mean?" It was Roger Pym, a little drunk, very objectionable.

"Yes," she said. "That, too. Perhaps you will have gathered by now that we have to treat Greg Franks' death as

54

suspicious. There was no question that it was not an accident. So at the very least you're all witnesses in a murder enquiry.''

"And suspects?" Roger Pym interrupted again. "I suppose we're all suspects, too."

"Yes," she said. "I suppose you are."

"Can we go, then?" Jane Pym said. The skin on her face seemed to have tightened, so the ridge of cheekbone under her eyes was sharp and noticeable, and her cheeks were thin and drawn.

"Yes," Claire said. "Go to bed. I'll come back early tomorrow to take statements."

Perhaps by then I'll feel more confident, she thought. I'll know how to cope with you.

"All except Mr. Palmer-Jones and Mr. Earl," she added. "I'd like to talk to you now."

They filed obediently and helplessly away. At the door Rose paused, and for a moment it was the old Rose who thought that everyone who came to the house needed her care.

"If you'd like anything to eat or drink," she said, "there's plenty in the kitchen. Just help yourself."

Surprised, Claire looked up and nodded, but she said nothing until the door had closed and she was left with the sergeant and the two men.

Molly hoped that Claire Bingham would shake George from his apathy. On their return to Myrtle Cottage from the *Jessie Ellen* he had been engrossed in his notebook. Sketching the new petrel, adding minute details, checking other species in Rose's books. It was as if what she thought of as the seawatching madness was still with him. He was brooding and absorbed.

She had succeeded at last in getting him to herself by volunteering to make coffee and forcing him into the kitchen to help.

"You do realise that Greg must have been pushed?" Molly said as she spooned coffee haphazardly into a jug. "Otherwise, how did his bag and the rest of his equipment go missing? He hadn't taken that on deck with him. That was no accident."

"No," George had said. "Probably not."

"Well," she said, "what are we going to do about it?"

"Nothing," he said. "It's nothing to do with us now. We'll cooperate fully with the police, tell the inspector everything we know, then leave the rest to her."

"What about Mr. and Mrs. Franks?" she demanded. "Don't you think we owe something to them?"

He looked at her, distant and surprised. "No," he said. "I don't think we do."

Molly began to clatter mugs and spoons onto a tray. His detachment, his cool assumption that Muriel and Dennis Franks were not worth bothering about, that they were, if anything, less important than his precious seabirds, infuriated her. It was not particularly that she wanted to meddle in the case. She did not need that sort of drama. It was that she worried about him. She knew he was trying to protect himself from the destructive guilt and depression which sometimes haunted him but could tell that the self-deception would not work. She thought he should do something. He should take the risk.

"I think you should go to see the Franks," she said. "They'll want to know what happened. It will make things easier for them."

He looked at her.

"I don't know what happened," he said. "I should only be in the way."

"No!" she cried. "Trust me! I'm right about this." As she spoke, she knew she sounded like a domineering nanny—a type of woman she detested.

"I'm afraid," he said, "that I've done enough damage."

"You can't think that Greg was murdered because we were there on the *Jessie Ellen* to look for him?"

"No," he said. "Perhaps not."

But she knew that in a sense he did feel responsible for Greg's death, and that if he did not become involved in the search for his murderer, the guilt would remain with him forever.

Molly did not like Claire—she thought she was bossy, overcontrolled—but hoped she would force George to look again at what had occurred on the boat. It would be impossible then for him to pretend that the only thing to have happened of any significance was the discovery of a new seabird.

When most of them filed out of the room, Claire felt more competent and businesslike. It was a room she felt comfortable in. If she lived in a cottage in the country, she would probably have decorated it like this, with white walls and stripped pine. It lacked imagination, and she could believe it belonged to her.

"I presume you have a list of all your clients," she said briskly to Rob.

"Yes," he said. "I thought you'd need it." He handed her a typed list. She looked at it quickly.

"Most of the people here give an address in Avon or Somerset," she said. "Was that a coincidence?"

"I don't think so," he said. "We're based in Bristol and do a lot of local advertising."

"Greg Franks gave an address in Bristol," she said. "The police have been there, but his parents say he hasn't lived at home for some time. You haven't anything more recent for him?"

"No," Rob said. "I presume he's been living in the city somewhere. I've seen him at a couple of bird club meetings."

"Did you know him well?"

"Not really," Rob said. "Whenever I went to see a bird, he was there. We'd talk, maybe go for a beer; then I might not see him again for months. That's how it is with a lot of serious birders."

"I see," she said, but she did not understand the obsession which was the only thing these men had in common. Besides, she would never allow such a chaotic arrangement to rule her social life.

"What work did he do?" she asked. "His parents were rather vague. He must have had some sort of regular employment to afford a car, a holiday like this."

Rob shrugged. "Perhaps," he said, "he had other ways of making money."

"What do you mean?"

"There were always rumours."

"What about?" she asked sharply. "Drugs? Was he a dealer?"

"That was what people said."

"But that didn't prevent you from allowing him onto the trip?"

"No," Rob said. "Of course not. They were only rumours. Besides, it's not something I feel strongly about."

The inspector looked at him sharply, wondering if he were trying to outrage her, but he was concentrating on rolling a very thin cigarette, and she could not tell.

"Was anyone absent from the deck in the time between Franks' going to lie down and your realising he was missing?" she asked.

"You must be joking!" Rob said. "I mean, I was looking at a bird which has certainly never been seen before in the western Palearctic and probably never in the world. I didn't notice anything but that beautiful dark rump and those bloody big feet. I do have some sense of priority."

His ridicule confused her. She did not have any idea what he was talking about. She turned to George.

"Mr. Palmer-Jones?" she asked with reverence and great hope.

"No," he said. "I'm sorry. I didn't notice anyone missing. As soon as we spotted what was obviously a very rare bird, there was a great deal of confusion. Everyone was concentrating on the sea."

She stared sadly at her small polished fingernails, and he saw that he had let her down. She turned to Rob.

"Who knew that Mr. Franks would be on the trip?" she asked. "Did anyone ask to see a passenger list before boarding?"

"No," Rob said. "Only George." He grinned wickedly.

"Is that relevant?" George asked. "I don't see, you know, how the murder can have been premeditated. None of us knew that Greg would feel seasick. In normal circumstances he would have been with us throughout the journey. It would have been impossible to kill him then."

"Not necessarily," she said so sharply that contradiction

58

was impossible. This was her case, and she was determined to control it in her own way. She turned again to Rob Earl.

"Tell me about Louis Rosco," she said. "How did you come to charter his boat? Did you go in recommendation or take up references?"

"It was more informal than that," Rob said. "He's a friend of Rose's. We met here. He gave me the names of some divers he'd taken out, and I checked with them. They said he was very good. He showed me round the boat. It seemed just what we wanted."

"Do you know anything more about him?"

"No. He doesn't talk about himself at all."

There was a silence. She suddenly wanted to be at home with Richard. Where there was no need to pretend to be hard and competent. She pushed away the moment of self-doubt.

"You can go to bed now," she said curtly. "I'll talk to you again in the morning."

Rob Earl stood up slowly and left the room. George remained seated.

"Inspector," he said, "there are some things you should know."

He explained about his agency and how he had been hired by the Franks to find their son. The information was almost more than she could take in.

"What do you intend to do now?" she asked.

He paused. "My wife thinks it would be . . ." He hesitated again. ". . . courteous, professionally correct, to visit the Franks, to explain personally as much as we know. I don't want to interfere in your investigation."

She looked at him with something approaching disappointment. He was grey, upright, old. She had told him that he had been a hero of hers, and that had been true. Now she only thought he was harmless. Well, she thought defensively, she was too grown up for heros now.

"I've no objection to your visiting the Franks," she said. "They've obviously been informed of their son's death, but I can see it might be helpful to them to talk to someone who was on the boat. Would you be able to do it in a day?"

"Yes," he said. He thought he would not want to be away

longer than that. It was the end of August, and a high-pressure system over Europe would mean migrant birds in the valleys. The intrusion of the thought shamed him, and he said nothing.

She stood up and smoothed the seams of her skirt.

"If you discover anything," she said, "I'll expect you to pass the information onto me."

But she smiled, and he thought the words were added out of kindness rather than any expectation that he would achieve anything. She was humouring him. He nodded sadly and thought that at least Molly would be pleased. Claire and Berry left the room before he did, and he stood there until he heard her car move up the valley to the main road.

When Claire Bingham got home, there was still a light in the living room. Richard had not drawn the curtains, and through the big picture window, which gave such a wonderful view over the harbour, she saw her husband asleep on the settee. The television was flickering with the black-and-white images of an old movie. Claire left Richard sleeping and went upstairs to Tom's room. She lifted him from his cot and cuddled him, smelling the baby powder, the clean soapy scent of him. He hardly stirred, and when she set him back under the cover, he was still asleep. When she woke Richard, he was surprisingly kind to her. Perhaps he recognised her tension. He made her tea, and they drank it together in bed.

In the Palmer-Jones bedroom in Myrtle Cottage it was cooler than in the rest of the house. The walls were thick and had kept out much of the heat of the day. The sash window was open, and the drawn curtains moved occasionally. Molly was in one of the twin beds reading by a low, heavily shaded lamp. She wore a nightshirt with a huge picture of Mickey Mouse on the front, a present from one of their children after a trip to the States. The children never gave him frivolous presents, he thought. Perhaps he had taken their education too seriously, and they thought him humourless and stern. Molly set down her book and waited for him to speak.

"I'm going to the Franks," he said. "Tomorrow morning. Do you want to come?"

"No," she said. "I've been thinking about it. It would be better if you went by yourself."

"Why?"

"I'm not sure about that inspector," she said. "I don't think she'll get anywhere with these people."

"And you will?" he demanded.

She ignored the sarcasm. "Yes," she said. "At least I know how to listen. People will talk to me."

She was right. She could sit next to a stranger and, with a quiet and sympathetic energy, charm from him confidences, anxieties, a full life story. It was because she was interested, she said. Most professional listeners weren't really. Doctors, social workers, teachers asked intimate questions, then used most of their brains to think about what they would have for tea. Professional detachment they called it.

"Why are you bothering with all this?" he said. "It's nothing to do with us. Not now. Leave it to the inspector."

"No!" she said, leaning forward, so the big Mickey Mouse on the front of the shirt wrinkled and seemed to be frowning.

"Greg Franks was a drug dealer!" he said. "Did you realise that?" When she was a social worker, Molly had worked with addicts. He had heard her wish a more violent death than drowning on the dealers who supplied them.

"No," she said, "but that makes no difference. We have to know who killed him. You don't understand. Whatever you say, we are involved. You involved us by agreeing to come here. You were involved by those blasted seabirds."

And then there was nothing he could say except that at least the trip to Bristol would give him the opportunity to go to the museum to look at their collection of birds' skins.

Rose stood quite still in Matilda's bedroom. It was directly above the living room, and she heard the muffled voices of the people who remained there. The windows were open, and occasionally she caught a full phrase usually spoken by the policewoman, whose voice was clear and shrill.

The baby was asleep on her side, with one hand stretched above her head beyond the bars of the cot. The room was lit by a low light, and in the corners there was shadow and the faint, mysterious movement of a ceramic mobile hung from the ceiling. Rose stroked the extended hand of the baby, then stood at the window staring out towards the sea.

She heard the door open but did not look around. She knew it would be Gerald. He had been following her around all evening offering affection, comfort, love. She found his loyalty touching, but she was not sure she could face him now. She had come to the baby's room to be alone.

"Rose," he whispered. He thought she would resent the intrusion, but the sense of her across the room made him feel heady and reckless. All the old dreams of marriage, of settling down with her, becoming a family, returned to him. He had never wanted her so much. "I came to see if there was anything I could do."

She turned to face him because she had come to believe that unkindness was worse than anything, and she did not want to hurt him. He saw that she was crying.

"Oh, Gerald," she said. "Dear Gerald. I don't know what to do. Everything's such a mess."

It had never before in any situation occurred to him that she might need him. She had been the determined one who held her family and business together, who made her own decisions. She had been the one who cheered him out of his loneliness and laughed at his weakness. He felt suddenly very strong and hopeful.

He moved to the window to stand beside her.

"It'll be all right," he said awkwardly, putting his arms around her, touching the bare skin of her shoulder, stroking it. "We're tired. It's the shock. We're all upset about Greg."

"I'm not upset," she said. He thought, looking at her so closely, at the lines around her eyes, the strain in her dark and heavy face, that she must be older than he. He had always thought of himself as boringly middle-aged in comparison to her, and the idea was flattering. He felt she had paid him a compliment. "I'm not upset," she said again. "Don't you understand? I'm bloody relieved that he's not around to trouble us anymore."

She laid her head on his shoulder, and for a moment Gerald stood in the warm half light of the nursery, quite content.

It seemed a moment of great promise and significance, the beginning of something magnificent. He had never been happy before.

Then Rose broke away. She did it gently, because even in her distress she could not bring herself to be unkind. She took his hands in hers and lifted them away from her body.

"Look," she said. "This won't do. It isn't fair. You'll have to go."

"No," he cried. "I want to be with you. I want to help."

"No one can do that now," she said, and took his hand again and led him to the door and sent him away.

She returned to the window, listening again to the voices of the people in the room below, trying to hear where their conversation might be leading. Soon after, the voices stopped. There were footsteps, the front door shutting, and the sound of a car engine being started. The headlights were reflected on the dense green leaves, and the car moved up the valley.

It was what Rose had been waiting for. She thought that now she was safe. She assumed that both police officers had left Porthkennan. In her anxiety and need for reassurance Inspector Bingham's promise to leave a policeman to "keep an eye on them" was forgotten.

She left the baby's room and walked carefully downstairs. At the front door she paused to make sure the house was quiet. She did not want Gerald and his clumsy sympathy again that night. Outside, she listened again, but there was only the screech of a tawny owl hunting on the moor by the tin mine, and she began to follow the lane down the valley. She was wearing no shoes, and the tarmac road outside the house, which had been unbearably hot during the day, was pleasantly warm. Even in the dark she could follow the path without a torch. She avoided the worst of the bramble and nettle.

When she reached the water, it was high tide, and the shingle beach was covered. As she approached the door of Rosco's cottage, she could feel the spray on her face from the waves breaking over the bigger rocks. Before she reached the house, she knew it was empty, and the unexpected stillness made her panic. She had hoped to see the lantern hanging from the hook in the low ceiling and Louis in the low chair by the window waiting for her, patient, calm, unassuming. In the past he always had been, and she realised how much she had taken him for granted. She opened the door and called inside to him, even went into the bedroom to see if he was sleeping there, but she knew from the beginning it was useless, and she would have to return to Myrtle Cottage disappointed.

Berry, who had followed her with interest down the lane and had suffered the blackthorn and bramble scratches patiently to have his curiosity rewarded, sensed her frustration as she passed quite close to him on her way back to the big house. She had not come to Rosco's to make a casual, friendly call or even, he thought, to discuss what had happened to Greg Franks. They were obviously what he, in his old-fashioned way would have called "romantically attached." Claire Bingham would have said they were lovers.

Claire Bingham would probably have taken the opportunity to go into the unlocked cottage and to search it, though she, too, had a healthy respect for rules. It never crossed Berry's mind. They had no search warrant, and he had not obtained permission of the owner. Perhaps it would not have made much difference if he had gone inside. In that light, with only a torch to search with, there was no guarantee that he would have found the gun, hidden as it was between the mattress and the metal frame of Rosco's bed. Even if he had defied the rule, there was no certainty that things would have been different. At the time he was more concerned about the woman. She seemed so frantic, almost haunted. So he just made sure that the door of Rosco's house was firmly secure and followed her back up the path to Myrtle Cottage.

6

Claire Bingham left home on Sunday morning while Richard was still sleeping. She knew it was a kind of escape. She hoped to avoid his tantrums about missing squash, the wheedling persuasion, the inevitable guilt. The guilt came all the same, as it always did with the joyous freedom which hit her as soon as she left the muddle of the house to begin work. The joy and the guilt were inseparable.

She had woken up early and lay, quite still so she would not disturb Richard, thinking of the Franks murder. It seemed to her now that Palmer-Jones had been right, and it was unlikely that the murder was premeditated. If anyone had planned to kill the young man, they would surely have chosen somewhere less public, less exposed. Was the crime then purely opportunistic, a spur-of-the-moment decision to settle an old score? Or had something happened on Friday night or Saturday morning to drive someone to murder? In any event, Claire thought it inevitable that murderer and victim must be previously known to each other. Franks might have been irritating and objectionable but would have been unlikely to drive a total stranger to such violence.

So, she decided as she showered and dressed, the aim of her interviews at Porthkennan would be to trace any connection between Greg and the other passengers and to reconstruct in detail all that had happened after the birdwatchers had joined the boat. It seemed simple and straightforward. She drank hot coffee too quickly, then drove fast down the harbour road, past the *Jessie Ellen*, still moored at the quay. She felt vigorous and refreshed.

Before leaving Heanor, she collected Berry from his parents' home. He had been relieved from surveillance duty outside Myrtle Cottage in the early hours of the morning by another detective, and Claire had arranged to pick him up. Many of the terraced houses in the street where he lived had been bought by hopeful immigrants from the north and turned into guest houses. In some cases the hopes had obviously not been realised; even on this bank holiday weekend hand-painted signs advertised that there were still vacancies.

Through large bay windows Claire saw tired landladies preparing for breakfast, setting ketchup bottles on plastic tablecloths, pouring sugar into plastic bowls.

In the car Berry told her about Rose's walk to the cottage on the shore.

"What was she after?" Claire asked.

"Him, I think," Berry said. "Rosco."

"They seem an unlikely sort of pair," she said, unconvinced.

"All the same," he said, "I think that's how it is."

When they arrived at Myrtle Cottage, Claire decided to interview Rose first. Whatever the reason for her midnight wander down the valley, it was a sign of panic. She thought the woman would be ready to talk.

For their interview they used the dining room, which was at the back of the house, cool and shady, a little gloomy. The light was filtered through the overgrown shrubs, planted too close to the window in the garden beyond. The furniture was dark and heavy and looked as if it had been inherited from an elderly relation. The room was rarely used.

"Mrs. Pengelly," Claire Bingham began.

"Miss," Rose interrupted. "I've used my maiden name since my divorce."

"Ah, yes." Claire looked at a piece of paper in a brown file. "When was that?"

"Twelve years ago," Rose said.

"You have lived in Myrtle Cottage since that time?"

Rose nodded. There was a silence which she felt expected

to fill. "It was left to my husband by his grandmother," she said. "When I met him, he was an actor in a small community theater group. He did a bit of writing and directing, too. Then he was offered the opportunity of working in London. Things hadn't been brilliant between us, and I certainly didn't want to move out of Cornwall, so we separated. Later he fell in love with a young actress, and we divorced. It was all quite friendly. When he went, I had two small children, so I stayed in the house. He's doing rather well now, and he's quite happy for me to stay here."

"Have you seen your husband recently?" Claire asked.

"Not since the children were old enough to travel to London by themselves. He used to come to Porthkennan to collect them for holidays, but they're both at college in town now, and he sees more of them now than I do."

There was another pause. Rose remained resolutely quiet.

"You have another child," the inspector said. "A baby."

"Yes," Rose said defiantly. "Matilda. She's eight months old."

She waited for the other, more awkward questions, but none came. At last Claire smiled and changed the direction of the conversation. She was enjoying herself. She felt in perfect control of the interview.

"How well did you know Greg Franks?" she asked.

"Not well at all. He stayed here occasionally if he was on his way to the Scillies, or if there was a particularly rare bird in the valley."

"Did he always come alone?"

"No. I can't remember him coming on his own before. There was usually a gang of them. Once he came with a girl."

"What was her name?"

"Victoria," Rose said. "It seemed rather inappropriate. Anyone less Victorian it would be hard to imagine. I never knew her surname."

"Tell me what happened on Friday night after you all arrived on the boat," Claire asked. "In as much detail as you can remember."

"It's very hard," Rose said. "It all seems rather a muddle,

as if it was a long time ago, and I found a lot of the conversations hard to understand. I enjoy watching birds, but I'm not in the same league as Rob or Roger. I don't suppose I have their passion."

"Start with the facts," Claire said. "What did you do when you first came aboard?"

"We stood at the deck rail for a while," Rose said. "Then we went into the saloon. Freddy had made supper sandwiches and pasties. There was beer. Everyone drank a lot of beer."

"And they talked about birds?" Claire asked.

"Of course they talked about birds. They were very tense, somehow, very anxious. Everyone's nerves seemed on edge. They were worried, I think, that after all the effort of the trip there would be nothing to see."

"How could you tell they were tense? Were there arguments?"

"There was a silly scrap between Roger and Greg about lists. Greg was just being mischievous, winding Roger up. Anyone with any sense could tell that. He implied that he'd seen more birds in Britain than Roger, but when we asked him outright how big his list was, he only laughed. 'I don't know,' he said. 'I'm a world-list man myself. I'll count up and let you know in the morning.' It seems juvenile now, but we were all short-tempered. It was very hot in that saloon. It seemed impossible to breathe. And we'd all had too much to drink. I was afraid there might even be a fight."

"But there wasn't a fight?"

"No," Rose said. "I've just explained, Greg turned the whole thing into a joke."

"What else happened?" the inspector asked lightly. "Any more dramas?"

"Jane Pym had more to drink than anyone," Rose said. Usually she would have considered this conversation gossip and hated herself for taking part in it. Now she thought self-preservation was more important. She would tell the inspector everything she wanted, to direct the interview away from her and Louis Rosco. "She was in a foul mood when she arrived. I think she and Roger had been rowing in the car on the way down. I don't blame her. He can't be an easy man to live with. Suddenly, after supper, when we were in the saloon, she turned to Greg Franks and accused him of being a criminal.''

Rose paused. I sound like one of those shop assistants in Woolworth's, she thought, who stand talking all day, trying to create excitement out of the boring details of their lives. But what, after all, is more exciting than murder?

"What do you mean?" the inspector asked, and Rose continued in the same gushing gossip's tone.

"She was really quite aggressive. It wasn't like Jane at all. Usually she's so quiet and controlled. You can never tell what she's thinking. It's her work, I suppose. 'Don't I know you?' she said. Greg told her she'd probably seen him birding. 'No,' she said. 'I've met you at work. Have you ever been on probation?' I thought he'd be upset, but he seemed to think the idea was hilarious. 'Not me,' he said in a clowning sort of voice. 'I've never been caught.' ''

"What did Mrs. Pym say then?"

"Nothing. I think she realised Greg had made a fool of her. She didn't say anything else all evening."

"Whose idea was it to hire the *Jessie Ellen* for the sea-watching trips?"

"Mine, I suppose," Rose said. "Rob Earl had run a couple of trips here in the autumn, and he was keen to try a pelagic. He asked if I knew anyone. Louis had moved into the valley, and I suggested him. Rob seemed very impressed. I just introduced them."

"Did you know that Mr. Rosco has served a prison sentence for a serious offence?"

"Yes," Rose said.

"Has he ever talked to you about it?"

"Not in detail. He said he had never intended it to end like that. He was too gullible, he said. It had been a means to an end."

"What did he mean by that?"

"I don't know," Rose said. "He doesn't like talking about it."

"Did Mr. Rosco ever meet Mr. Franks here?"

69

"No," Rose said. "He didn't like the birdwatchers much. He kept out of the way when they were here."

"Did he know that Greg Franks would be aboard the *Jessie Ellen* with this party? Did Mr. Earl send him a passenger list?"

"No, he had very little to do with the passengers. He only needed to know how many there would be."

The inspector looked at a sheet of paper in the file. It was an indication, Rose thought, that the interview was almost over.

"Did you like Greg Franks, Miss Pengelly?"

"No," Rose said. "I thought he was cocky, irritating, rude. Some people may have found him amusing. I thought he was offensive."

"Oh," the inspector said. "How did he offend you?"

"There was nothing specific," Rose said. "It was his manner."

There was a silence. The inspector gathered her papers together. "Just one last thing," she said. "Why did you go to the cottage on the shore last night?"

Rose stared at her in shocked amazement, as if the woman had been gifted with supernatural powers. The inspector continued, "You did go, I presume, to see Louis Rosco."

Rose nodded.

"Why?"

"We're friends," Rose said. "I wanted to talk to him." She turned sharply to the detective. "Is he all right?" she said. "You haven't arrested him?"

"Why should we do that?" Claire asked.

Rose shook her head.

"No," Claire said. "We haven't arrested him. He spent the night on the boat. We'll be talking to him later today."

"He wouldn't have killed Greg Franks!" Rose cried. "What reason would he have?"

"Miss Pengelly," the inspector asked gently, formally, "is Louis Rosco the father of your child?"

Rose nodded, and Claire Bingham was left with the satisfaction of knowledge but with no clear idea of what the information added up to.

Jane Pym had slept heavily in a blank, unnatural stupour and woke slowly to a headache and a feeling of empty nausea. She thought for a moment she was in hospital waking up after an operation, and the reality came as a disappointment. It would have been wonderful to be in hospital in a state of sympathetic dependence.

Roger was already awake and on the telephone. He seemed to spend the whole of that day talking to seabird freaks about the red-footed petrel. He seemed to have taken possession of the bird, as if no one else was competent to deal with it, and managed to imply that he had found it and first realised its significance. When Jane emerged at last from the bedroom into the living room, he was talking in dreadful French to a professor who worked in the natural history museum in Paris. How he tracked down the home number of a Frenchman on a Sunday in August she never discovered. The arrival of the policewoman and the summons to the cool dining room to answer questions came almost as a relief. More than anything she would have preferred to be at work. If that was impossible, when she was called into the dining room, she was glad at least to escape Roger's gloating descriptions, the pseudoscientific jargon of bird identification, the strictures to secrecy. If Roger mentioned Greg Franks' death at all in these interminable phone calls, it was an inconvenience which prevented his carrying out proper research and put him at the mercy of others. She found the performance sickening.

Claire Bingham considered Jane Pym with suspicion. She did not, like some of her colleagues, think all probation officers were seditious and revolutionary, but she was wary of them. They were usually unreliable and unpredictable. They seemed to work alone, with no authoritative superior. And then there was, between the women, an element of competition. They stared at each other across the polished wooden table, each almost a mirror image of the other, angular, intense, frowning. Both women were used to conducting interviews. They knew the rules of the game. Neither would want to lose face.

"Why did you decide to come to Cornwall this week-end?" Claire asked.

"My husband had booked through Rob's company to go on the *Jessie Ellen* and to stay here for a few days afterwards. I decided to come with him."

"Do you usually accompany your husband on his bird-watching expeditions?"

"Not usually." She tried halfheartedly to explain. A degree of confession was expected in an interview like this. She was prepared to play the role for the inspector. "Look," she said. "Our marriage has been a bit shaky lately. Perhaps we both expect too much of each other. I wanted to make an effort. Birdwatching means so much to him. I wanted to show him I could try to share it." She paused. "I wish now, of course, that I had never come."

"How well did you know Greg Franks?" the inspector asked.

"Not at all," Jane Pym said, and then perhaps her interviewer's instinct, her sense that she might have been tricked, made her continue: "At least I think I may have met him, but I can't remember exactly where."

"On the *Jessie Ellen* you accused him of having been on probation," Claire said.

"It wasn't an accusation," Jane said. "I just had an idea that I'd met him professionally."

"Surely if he'd been on probation to you, you would have remembered him."

"Of course, though I've had a lot of clients over the years. But I prepare social enquiry reports on people going to court, and there have been hundreds like that. I see them for a couple of interviews, then never meet them again."

"I understand that he spent a couple of weeks in a probation hostel in Bristol when he was on bail. Could you have met him there?"

Jane remembered the big family house on the corner of the suburban road which managed to carry with it the air of an institution.

"Yes," she said, trying to picture Greg in the kitchen doing his turn at washing up, in one of the house meetings

72

baring his soul. "That's possible. I did a six-months' stint there about four years ago."

"What about Louis Rosco?" the inspector asked, and then echoing Jane's earlier words, mocking them, asked, "Could you have met him professionally?"

Jane looked at her sharply. "Has he been in trouble?" she asked.

The inspector nodded. "Why? Do you remember him?"

"No, but there's something about him that's familiar. Not about him personally, but the way he talks to people he doesn't know. He's suspicious. Has he been in prison?"

The inspector nodded again. "He completed his sentence in Leyhill Open Prison in Gloucestershire at about the same time as you were working in the hostel," she said. "You don't remember him?"

"No," she said, but the inspector, who was skilled at picking up these things, did not quite believe her and thought that she was being guided by a peculiar social workers' code of confidentiality. Claire thought it did not matter. The man's records would be available to them, and the name of his probation officer would be there. She turned back to Jane Pym.

"How did your husband get on with Mr. Franks?" she asked.

Jane shrugged. "They were friendly rivals," she said. "Roger has been birdwatching for a long time. He's seen a lot of birds in Britain. The younger twitchers were a little envious. Greg liked to think he was catching Roger up."

"Did you talk to Greg Franks after he went to sleep off his seasickness yesterday on the *Jessie Ellen*?" Claire asked.

"No," Jane said. "Of course not. What on earth would I have to talk to him about?"

Then she sat in a calm, detached way smoking a cigarette and waited for the inspector to tell her that the interview was at an end.

When she had spoken to Jane Pym, the inspector sent Berry to the car to radio the police station. Her superintendent had promised to contact Customs & Excise and the Drugs Squad to see if they had information on Greg Franks.

But now, too, there should be more details on the Louis Rosco case. Claire did not have much faith in her superintendent's abilities as an investigator but acknowledged that he was a good liaison man. He seemed to have friends in every force in the country. She never asked how he managed it but was willing to use the information he provided.

Berry walked through the house and out into bright sunlight. Swallows were gathering in clouds in the valley and perching on the telegraph wire along the road preparing for the migration south. On a white bench outside the cottage Rose Pengelly was sitting, barefoot and brown legged, like a Gypsy, with the baby at her breast. Unembarrassed, he continued towards the car. In the house the phone rang. Berry thought it might be the superintendent and turned back to answer it, but Roger Pym had already picked up the receiver, and Berry heard him say to no one in particular, "It's Tim Robertson from Madeira."

When the sergeant returned to the dining room, he was carrying coffee in big earthenware mugs shaped like flowerpots.

"Miss Pengelly thought we might like this," he said.

"Well?" the inspector demanded, refusing to be distracted, irritated by his lack of urgency, by the time he had been away. "What have we got?"

"Greg Franks was well known to the customs investigations department," he said, spooning brown sugar in his coffee. "They're a bit upset. They were all set up for a big operation. They hoped he might lead them to the organiser. He was certainly a courier, they say. Probably a small-time dealer, too. They're interested, of course, in all his contacts and would like to see his diary or address book if we find one."

"We've got to find a home for him first," she said. "We know he hadn't been living at his parents' house for months. That's why they hired George Palmer-Jones. We can't trace him by his belongings because apparently they all went overboard when he did." She drank the coffee in small, polite sips and continued thinking aloud. "Perhaps that's the significance of the missing bag and equipment," she said. "Perhaps the murderer threw it away to stop anyone finding out where Greg had been living. It's interesting that he was killed after the first serious attempt to trace him."

"Mr. Palmer-Jones didn't seem to think he'd have any problem discovering Franks' address," Berry said. "He told me that these twitchers all keep in touch with each other by phone. It was just a question of asking one of them for Greg's phone number and tracing the address from that."

"Well," she said, "Roger Pym is one of these twitchers, isn't he? Lets have him in and see if he knows where Franks has been hiding."

Roger Pym was nervous. He talked too much and waved his arms. He insisted over and over again how upset he was by Greg's death. He had known the boy for a long time, he said. Since he was a youngster. In fact, he thought he could take the credit for starting Greg Franks on his birdwatching career. He hadn't actually taught Greg, but the lad used to hang around with some of his pupils at school.

"Have you seen him around lately?"

"Of course. He was a serious twitcher. I see him at most of the rare birds which turn up in the country."

"You never met him socially?"

"Good Lord, no! We'd have nothing in common."

"Your wife described you as friendly rivals. Would that be accurate?"

A touch of annoyance, of vanity, crossed his face, and she thought for a moment he intended to contradict her, but he laughed with a forced aimability and said yes, that would probably be right. She had probably heard about their little argument on the boat. It was Greg teasing, of course. There was absolutely no possibility that Greg could have seen as many birds in the U.K. as he had. She took him through the events of the day before, and even to her he propounded the fantasy that he had found the unidentified petrel. Of course he hadn't spoken to Greg Franks, he said. There was too much going on. He hadn't left the deck for a moment.

"Could you give me Mr. Franks' telephone number?" the

inspector asked. "I understand that birdwatchers keep in frequent touch on the phone."

The question startled Pym. For the first time in the interview he was quiet. Then the words started again, fast, jumbled, nervous. No, he said, he was sorry but he didn't have Greg's latest number. He had the old one, of course, for his parents' home but nothing recent.

"Isn't that unusual?" the inspector asked.

"Not really," he said. "Not now. There's Birdline, a telephone answering service, and the old grapevine is dead."

"So you don't know where he had been living recently?" she asked, though by now the young man's address had become such a mystery that she no longer expected a positive answer.

"In Bristol," Roger Pym said. "I'm sure he was living in Bristol. But not his exact address. No."

Late in the morning the superintendent arrived. Not, Claire thought, to offer assistance, to accept some of the responsibility in a difficult case, but to check up on her and because the trip to Porthkennan would be a pleasant break from the office before he went home for Sunday lunch. He was Cornish, a great bull of a man, wide, neckless, with a big, square head. His name was Wargan.

"Well," he said in his growling voice, "How's it going?"

She shook her head. "No one will admit to speaking to him on the boat yesterday after he went to lie down," she said. "They all seem to have been so excited about this rare bird that they took no notice of anything. The probation officer, Mrs. Pym, thinks she might have come across him at work, possibly when he was at a probation hostel on bail. Can we check their records on that?"

"No," Wargan said, finding apparent satisfaction in making the investigation more difficult and complicated for her. "I phoned them this morning. There was a fire at the hostel. I checked the date of the fire with our records on Franks. It will have been while he was on bail. The place was gutted, and all their records were lost."

"What sort of fire?" she asked. "Arson?" It was, she thought, a coincidence. Rosco had been convicted of arson.

He shook his head. "Apparently not. There was a detailed investigation, and they found it was started by an electrical fault."

"Have you got an address for Franks yet?" the inspector asked. "No one here seems to know where he'd been living since he left his parents."

The superintendent shook his head. "He seems to have disappeared from all the official records about a year ago," he said. "He hasn't claimed dole or social security in that time, and he hasn't paid tax or national insurance. The car he was driving was registered and insured in his father's name. We'll put out a press statement this afternoon and get his picture in the papers tomorrow. Someone will know where he's been living."

He would enjoy doing that, Claire thought. Wargan always got on well with the media. He especially liked being on local television news, smiling roguishly at the female interviewer, developing his accent so nobody could mistake him for an incomer.

Berry had been sitting apart, listening to the conversation. Now, for the first time he spoke. "What about Louis Rosco?" he said. "Is he still on the *Jessie Ellen*? Should we get a search warrant and go over his cottage before he comes back?"

Wargan shook his head. "No need for that," he said. "We know that the first time Franks and Rosco met this weekend was at Heanor, and Rosco's been under observation since then. There can't possibly be anything belonging to Franks in the cottage. They've done a thorough search of the boat now and found nothing there. Rosco can go home as soon as he wants to, though I think we should have him in to the station later for questioning. He's your most likely suspect, isn't he? He's killed a man once." He nodded towards the dining room door. "I can't imagine any of that bunch out there having the guts. Still, it's your case."

So a second opportunity to search the cottage on the shore

77

was missed. When the police made a connection between Franks and Rosco, they searched the cottage, but then they were looking for drugs. By that time, the gun lying between the lumpy flock mattress and the metal frame of the bed had been moved, and they found nothing.

7

Duncan James spent the day outside, waiting with mounting panic for the summons to the dining room to be questioned. At least in the garden, with its open view down the valley, he could fight off the claustrophobia which had been tormenting him since he had gone below deck on the *Jessie Ellen* to sleep. His father had worked as a young man in a tin mine, and whenever Duncan thought of the working conditions he must have endured, he felt ill. Claustrophobia had dominated Duncan's childhood and altered his life. The irrational fear of dark, damp places had been one of the spurs to his academic success. It had sent him from Cornwall to civilised inland Britain. It had made him cautious and thrifty. The tin mine represented insecurity, poverty, failure.

Now he was back in Cornwall, and the childhood fear had returned. In the bunkroom across the yard he had slept badly, and when he did drift into unconsciousness, he dreamed of drowning in dark cold water. Even in daylight in the sunny garden, the memory of the dream returned. He tried to banish it by thinking of Anne at home in Somerset with the children and, by an effort of will, maintained a degree of equilibrium and calm.

He could not remember being happy before he knew Anne. They had met at university. She had been an undergraduate, and he had been doing post-doctoral research and a little teaching. He had seen her first when he had taken a small group into some beech woods to collect fungi for identification. The colour of the beech woods and her hair and her smile still glowed in his memory. He had known even then on the first meeting that she was special. She had changed him in a month. His colleagues told him that she had made him human. Before Anne he had been notorious for his bad temper and his unwillingness to compromise. Suddenly he found a sense of humour.

Duncan did not dare ask her to marry him until she had completed her degree. Then he needed several drinks to give him the courage to make the proposal, and he had botched it with his shyness, so in the end she had proposed to him. Afterwards he had been too excited to sleep for a week. He had wandered round the university in dazed and bedraggled confusion while she made the arrangements for the wedding. If he had understood more clearly the difference in their backgrounds, it might never have taken place. In the classlessness of academic life it had not mattered. He realized that she never had to worry about money, that she had been to a boarding school, that her father had some land in the West Country, but at university everyone's parents seemed wealthier than his had been. There had even been a certain status in being poor. He had imagined, if he thought about it, that her father was a farmer.

She bullied him once, soon after they met, to take her to Cornwall to show her where he had been brought up. It was late autumn, raining, and the weekend was a bleak anticlimax. His parents, who had been older than most of his friends' parents, were dead, and there were no other relatives to introduce her to. He showed her the rented cottage where he had lived as a child, and she made no comment then, no comparison with her own home. It was only after they were engaged that she drove him to meet her parents in Gloucestershire, and when he saw where they lived, he thought at first she was playing a trick on him. The long drive, the acres of garden, the house so old and grand that he might have been taken there as a schoolboy on an educational visit, astounded him. There were two farms on the estate and a gamekeeper; most of the village was dependent on Anne's father for employment. It almost wrecked the relationship. For a time he lost all his confidence in her. He thought he must have misjudged her. Because she was rich, he supposed she must be different. Then she persuaded him that was ridiculous, and at last the old happiness returned. It was only later, when they were married, that he discovered that his fear had been justified and that in some important things she *was* different.

Now, sitting in the garden waiting for the ordeal of being questioned, he tried not to blame Anne for the mess he was in. He knew it was all his own fault.

The police kept him waiting all morning, and he wondered in the heightened state of nervous panic if they had done that on purpose to frighten him. It was early afternoon when Berry came to find him. The policeman saw a large, uncoordinated man walking backwards and forwards along the overgrown path by the stream. He was dressed with an old-fashioned shabbiness, and when Berry called to him, he turned with a sad and frightened look, like a child asking a stern parent not to deal with him too harshly. When Duncan was led into the sudden shadow of the dining room, he blinked short-sightedly and peered unhappily towards the inspector. She had been disturbed by the superintendent's visit and the fact that they still had no recent address for Greg Franks. Her superiors would see that as incompetence, and she had wondered even if she should leave Berry to complete the statements while she devoted her energy to that. She had decided in the end to stay, but her attention was still on the problem of where Franks had been living, and her questions were mechanical and routine. She could not believe that this absentminded academic could help her.

"Dr. James," Inspector Bingham said, "why did you decide to come to Cornwall this weekend?"

"I was interested in the birdwatching element," he said. "I work as regional officer for the Nature Conservancy Council, but ornithology isn't really my subject. I thought this holiday would be an excellent introduction. My patch covers the whole of the south-west peninsula, and it did seem important to learn a little about seabird identification." He was rather proud of his answer, and it gave him confidence. Only the sergeant, sitting out of sight, half-hidden by a giant rubber plant, gave Duncan some cause for concern. He had calm blue eyes, and Duncan had a guilty sense that the sergeant could tell when he was lying.

"When did you decide to come to Heanor?" the inspector asked.

"Only last week," he said. "It was an impulse. I had a few days' leave to take. I was lucky there was still a place available."

"Yes," she said. "I see. How did you hear about the trip?"

"I'd read about them in the natural history press," he said. "They're quite famous, you know."

"Had you met Greg Franks before?"

"Not as far as I'm aware," Duncan said. "I may have met him through my work. I come across pressure groups and representatives of natural history societies occasionally, but having met Greg, I doubt if he was involved in that kind of thing. And besides, I think I should have remembered him if I'd seen him before. He was quite an exhibitionist."

There was a pause.

"What effect did that exhibitionism have on the other passengers?"

It was the sergeant who spoke, and Duncan found the question strangely disturbing.

"I don't know," he said lamely. "Franks seemed to take a delight in annoying them, but there was a lot of conversation I didn't understand. I hadn't met them before, you see, so it was difficult to gauge their reactions. There was some wrangling about lists. That seemed incomprehensible to me."

"Yesterday afternoon," the inspector said, "when Greg Franks told everyone he was going to lie down, the others say that they were too interested in the seabird to notice what was going on. But you tell me that you're not a birdwatcher, so you might have been more aware of other things. Did you go to see Greg during that time?"

"No," Duncan James said. "I quite forgot about him until later."

"You didn't notice anyone else move forward to the deck where he was sleeping?"

"No," James said. "I'm sorry. I was reading."

"But you did go to look for Greg when they found the rare bird?"

"Oh, yes," James said. "That's when I remembered him. And the others seemed so excited by the bird. They were afraid of missing anything. So I volunteered."

"Was everyone on the deck when you left?"

"I don't know." He allowed himself to play the part of vague, absentminded academic for all it was worth. "There was so much noise and confusion, you see."

"Yes," she said, "so I've been told. You didn't see anything unusual when you went to look for Greg?"

"No," he said, hesitating, "not at first. When he wasn't on deck, I supposed he was in his bunk. He had looked terribly ill. Then, when I went below, there was no sign of him. Nothing. Even his sleeping bag had disappeared."

"How long was it before you went back to the others to tell them he was missing?"

There was a hesitation, and though the inspector seemed not to notice, Duncan was aware of the sergeant's perceptive and compassionate gaze.

"I suppose it must have seemed rather a long time," Duncan said, "before I went back on deck. I looked in the places where he might have been. I thought he might have been sick in the lavatory or lying down in the saloon. It seemed inconceivable, of course, that he could have just have disappeared. When I did go back to the others, they didn't believe me."

"No," the inspector said.

He was still waiting for the awkward questions that he had been dreading and did not realise that the interview was over until the inspector asked if he would send Mr. Matthews in as he went out. His relief gave him courage, and at the door he hesitated.

"I'd like to get home as soon as possible," he said. "Would it be all right to go back tomorrow?"

The inspector looked up at him and smiled.

"I can't stop you, of course," she said. "But I'd rather you stayed here for a couple of days. You had planned to be here on holiday anyway, hadn't you?"

"Yes," he said. "Very well. I understand."

Only when he was outside the door, away from the steady stare of the sergeant, did he begin to shake uncontrollably.

Gerald Matthews repeatedly took off his spectacles and rubbed them with the hem of his jersey in what they thought was a gesture of nervousness and was in fact the result of a contained excitement. All day he had been even more aware than usual of Rose. He watched her from a distance, knowing that if he made a wrong move, the fragile understanding which he felt had spontaneously developed between them in Matilda's bedroom would be lost. He saw her for the first time as vulnerable, unhappy, obtainable. It never occurred to him that by offering her marriage now he would be exploiting her shock and sadness. He wanted her. The gentleness and tact he showed now in his discretion, in keeping his distance, was a tactic in obtaining her. Concern and consideration for her feelings had nothing to do with it.

He thought of Greg Franks' death with a celebratory joy. His problem was in trying to keep the emotion under control. He managed it by involving himself in Roger Pym's research into the possible identification of the petrel and channelled his excitement into that. Yet all the time he was watching Rose through the living room window, so in touch with her that he believed he could smell her hair and hear the peaceful breathing of the baby on her knee.

When Gerald Matthews was called into the dining room, he was aggressive and hostile. It was not exactly a performance—more a welcome opportunity to release the tension which had been building up all day. The inspector did not read too much into his reaction. He was the sort of man who would pride himself on complaining, on standing up for his rights. He was pale, slight, ageless. He would look much the same when he was fifty.

"Look!" he said. His voice was flat, hard, northern.

"What have you been doing to upset Rose Pengelly? She was nearly in tears when she came out of here."

"What does that have to do with you?" Claire asked. She smiled a cruel, tight-lipped smile. You're a failure, she thought. Rose Pengelly's chosen Rosco. Don't you know that yet?

"I'm her friend," Gerald Matthews said, blustering, hoping that he would be taken for Matilda's father. "A very special friend."

"You help her, do you? Support her in times of crisis?"

"That's right."

"Does she confide in you?"

"I hope so."

"Did she tell you, for example, who was the father of her child?"

"I didn't ask," he lied. "It was none of my business."

Claire smiled again, laid her palms deliberately on the table, and leaned forward. She wanted to show him who was in charge.

"Tell me about Greg Franks," she said.

"There's nothing to tell. I'd only met him a couple of times. He was not the sort of birdwatcher I approve of. He probably wouldn't even have called himself a birdwatcher. He would say he was a birder or a lister—dreadful Americanisms. He didn't know very much about common birds. These youngsters move onto rarities too quickly, in my opinion. They don't put in the groundwork. I'd been watching my local reed bed for years before I started going to the Scillies."

She considered his words as the ravings of a lunatic. She had no idea what he was talking about. But they all came back to these birds, she thought. Perhaps I'm missing something. Can they really matter in a case like this? She turned Gerald Matthews' attention back to Greg Franks.

"So you disapproved of him?"

"I did."

You were probably jealous of Franks, she thought, because he was young and irresponsible. He knew how to enjoy himself. It was hard to imagine Gerald Matthews as ever having been young, and she had by now gained an impression of Greg as a man who, above all things, knew how to enjoy himself.

"Apart from the birds," she said, "was there any reason for the disapproval?"

"I'd heard rumours," he said.

"About drugs?"

"Yes," he said. "And about other things. Everyone knew he was mixed up in something shady. It was as if they thought he was clever. 'Look at Greg Franks,' they'd say. 'Just back from Thailand,' or 'Just bought a new 'scope,' or 'Driving a new car.' 'Bet he didn't get that on the dole,' they'd say. It made me sick. I didn't think Rose should have him here. She agreed not to let him stay again, but here he was. She's too kindhearted."

"So you weren't expecting him to be here this weekend?"

"No," Gerald said sulkily. "It was a shock. I don't know what made her change her mind."

"Have you asked Miss Pengelly why she allowed him to come?" she asked. He muttered that it was none of his business, and she could do what she liked.

Molly Palmer-Jones spent all day listening. It was not exactly that she was eavesdropping. She was always in full view of the people who were talking. It was that they did not consider her worth bothering with. They thought she posed no threat. And the shock made them want to talk; they were glad to have someone sympathetic to share their worries with. When they came away from Molly, they felt better.

Even when she was in the shady dining room, she was listening—to the whispered conversation between the inspector and her sergeant that was taking place when she entered the room, and to the subtext beneath the questions, trying to follow the line of reasoning which prompted Claire Bingham to ask them. Molly was left with the disturbing impression that there was little logic, that the questions were a random, almost desperate attempt to find a previous relationship between Greg and the other passengers. It was clear already that there were no witnesses to the murder, or if anyone had seen anything suspicious, they were not admitting it.

All day Molly watched them, too. They might have thought she was asleep in the deck chair under the front porch, a book turned facedown on her knee. It would have been understandable. She was elderly and had been up for half the night. In fact, she had more stamina than any of them, and through half-closed eyes she watched them. From her raised position she could see Rose on her bench with the view of the valley, and she could tell that Rose was watching, too, and waiting for something. Each time a car approached, the younger woman became tense until it appeared through the vegetation, and then there was disappointment. She must have been able to identify Rosco's van just by the bangs and rattles as it came through the trees, because before she could see it, she had already relaxed. When she had seen it safely down the lane to the cottage on the shore, she felt able to leave her white bench and go inside to do other things.

Molly watched Duncan James waiting in the garden until it was his turn to be interviewed. She saw him stoop to examine the aquatic plants at the edge of the stream, as if the routine intellectual activity of identifying them would keep his mind from other, less pleasant things. And because the windows were open, she could hear what was going on inside the house, the constant telephone calls of Roger Pym, the surprising encouragement of Gerald Matthews, and the facetious mocking of Rob Earl.

When Rose took Gerald into the kitchen late in the afternoon to put things straight between them, she took no notice of Molly, dozing outside the open door. Even if the old lady did hear, she thought, what would it matter? It was time the thing was out in the open. It had been ridiculous to make a secret of it. Gerald went with her light-headedly. He had never felt so alive.

"I want to talk to you," Rose said. "It's about Tilly."

He was immediately wary, prepared for disappointment.

"What about her?"

"Louis is her father."

He said nothing but stared down the valley.

87

"You don't seem surprised," she said.

"I've seen you around together," he said. "You always seem very friendly." He did not tell her that he was so used to disappointment that even in the excitement of the morning he was preparing for it. He did not tell her that pride was all he had left, so he was not going to let her see how hurt he was. What about Greg Franks? he wanted to scream. Where did he come into all this? What was he doing here?

"There are things you don't know about Louis," she said. "Things you don't understand. When he first came to Porthkennan, he confided in me. I felt sorry for him."

"And isn't that what you felt for me?" he lashed out. "Poor old Gerald. No friends. So social graces. Isn't that what you thought? But you wouldn't let me go to bed with you."

"Gerald," she said, "I'm sorry." But as she was talking to him, she was looking outside, towards the shore.

"You should grow up," he shouted angrily. "We're not all lame dogs to be petted."

"I'm sorry," she said again, but the repeated apology only irritated him, and then he did ask the question that had been singing in his brain as a way of getting back at her.

"Where did Greg Franks come into all this?" he demanded. "What did you mean last night when you said he was upsetting things?"

She went suddenly white, as if he had slapped her face.

"Nothing!" she said, in a whisper, looking for the first time at Molly beyond the open door. "I didn't mean anything."

Roger Pym waited until the inspector returned to Heanor before he sought Molly out. Until he sat beside her, she had not realized how much pressure he was under. She had thought he was wrapped up in the new bird, but perhaps, after all, that was only a distraction. She had met him with George and had always dismissed him as insensitive, mindlessly competitive. She knew he taught physical education at a large comprehensive school on a council estate outside

88

Bristol and thought him obsessed with his own fitness and his own list. He would be the worst kind of gym teacher, she thought, concerned only to prove that he could run faster and longer distances than the boys in his charge. Now she saw he was getting older and thought that as it became less easy to compete, he would grow vicious. When he sat beside her, he was sweating. Beads of perspiration clung to the hairs on his arms, and he wiped his forehead with the back of his hand.

"This is terrible," Roger said. "I don't know what the school will say about my being mixed up with the police like this. Or the parents."

Roger's previous descriptions of the parents at his school had been a little prejudiced. They were feckless mothers who either drank or were on the game, and unemployed, illiterate fathers. Neither, Molly thought, would be particularly concerned about Roger Pym. She said it must be very worrying.

"There was that ridiculous argument about the list," Roger said. "Someone must have mentioned it to the police. I hope too much isn't made of it."

"Did you ever find out what Greg's list was?" Molly asked. It was a mischievous question. She did not expect a response.

"No," he cried, his hands shaking. "No. Of course not."

Jane Pym walked up, as cool and composed as if she were appearing in court. The police had given them permission to leave Porthkennan for an hour, she said. She quite fancied a drink, so why didn't they drive into Heanor and go to that place where they had spent so much of their honeymoon? Roger agreed immediately and was almost gallant.

They walked away, but Molly remained where she was. She hoped that Rose would want to talk to her, too. Her curiosity had been aroused by the overheard conversation. She had tantalising glimpses of the woman in the kitchen, peeling vegetables in preparation for supper. Molly wondered if she should call in and offer to help, but it seemed that Rose preferred to be alone while she mixed a crumble in a large brown bowl.

Duncan James had walked back to his position in the lower garden by the stream. As dusk approached, his claustrophobia returned, and he paced backwards and forwards trying to fight it off.

8

G*eorge* left Porthkennan early on Sunday morning and arrived in Bristol to quiet streets and the sound of church bells. The new development around the docks was empty. The wealthy young people who lived there would still be sleeping off the parties of the night before. There was an occasional jogger stumbling over the fancy cobbles on the path along the river. George considered parking there, finding somewhere for coffee. And still in the back of his mind was the wonder of the red-footed petrel, which seemed to grow larger and more vivid in his imagination, so he thought, too, of looking up the curator of vertebrate biology at the museum, who was an old friend of his. But he knew these were delaying tactics. Before he did anything, he would have to see the Franks.

He drove through the town centre and out to the suburbs beyond. There was a cemetery lined by dusty trees, and the only colour was on a flower stall outside the gates. It was a bank holiday weekend, and respectable citizens would be decorating, cleaning the car, or in caravans on the Welsh coast. The pavements and the roads were still almost empty, although the sun was shining and it was hotter than ever.

Muriel Franks opened the door to him. She was wearing a candlewick dressing gown and fluffy blue slippers. Her mouth was slightly open, and her face was grey. For a moment she seemed not to recognize him; then she considered him with a flat, expressionless stare.

"It's you," she said, and he could not tell what she thought about his appearing on the doorstep. "I thought it would be the police again. You'd better come in."

She stood aside, and he walked ahead of her into the stuffy sitting room. Dennis Franks sat in one of the large soft armchairs. He, too, looked exhausted, but he seemed sustained by a vague and undirected anger. When George came in, he stood up.

"You've got a nerve," he said, "coming here after what's happened."

"I thought you might like to talk to me," George said. "I was on the boat when Greg died."

"They won't bloody tell me what happened," Franks said with helpless fury. "They say there were suspicious circumstances. I don't know what that means."

He turned towards George in a threatening way, his chin thrust forward, hoping perhaps for an excuse for the relief of violence but not quite able to see it through. When he spoke again, it was with a confused desperation.

"What have you done?" he demanded. "You went to Cornwall to send my son home, and now he's dead."

Muriel Franks, who had followed George into the room and was sitting, crumpled, on a corner of the sofa, began to cry.

"I'm so sorry," George said, but he knew the words were inadequate, and his sympathy only seemed to refuel Franks' anger.

"What did you say to him?" the man cried. "Did you frighten him into jumping from the boat?" Then, because of his lack of control over his wife's tears illustrated his lack of control in the whole unbelievable situation he added, "Have you seen what this is doing to Muriel?"

George was becoming angry himself, with the police who seemed to have left the couple without any real information, with all their questions unanswered.

"Didn't the police tell you that they believe Greg was murdered?" George said.

"I've told you!" Franks cried. "They wouldn't bloody tell me anything. I want to know!"

Muriel Franks looked up, bewildered and unhappy, startled by the noise of his voice, and her words were so inappropriate and irrational that the two men stared at her for a moment in silence. "He was such a good little swimmer when he was a boy," she said. "I told the police that."

At last Franks sat beside her. "Why don't you go and lie down?" he said gently. "You must be tired."

But she shook her head and remained where she was.

"I'm afraid the swimming wouldn't have helped," George said. He felt Muriel deserved an explanation. "The police think he must have been unconscious when he reached the water."

"How!" Franks demanded.

"There's a head wound," George said, "which can't be explained by Greg's falling."

"Are you telling me that someone hit our lad on the head and no one stopped him? What the hell were you all doing?"

"We were all on deck birdwatching," George said. "Greg had been seasick and was lying down on his own." He knew how unlikely the explanation sounded. It was impossible to describe the noise and excitement of that time on the *Jessie Ellen*.

"I don't understand it," Franks went on raging at the mystery, the uncertainty. "It seems a strange do to me. I want to know what happened." He turned to George. "I hold you responsible," he said. "I was paying you. You owe me an explanation."

"You do realise," George said, "that there'll be a police investigation. The detective in charge of the enquiry seems very competent."

"I want you to find out what happened," Franks said. It was something to hold on to. "I've no control over the police. You'll be my man. I'll be paying you."

"I'll be my own man," George said, stung at last to retaliation, "whoever pays the bill. If I agree to help you, it'll be to find out what happened to Greg. And I'll do it my way."

Franks moved over to the window and stared out into the empty street. A woman pulling a fat corgi on a lead walked

93

past and peered in through the net curtains with a malevolent curiosity.

"All right," he said. His life had been ruled by certainty, the figures of profit and loss, the routine of production. In his own way he had been a powerful man. At least with George's intervention in the case, he would have the power of involvement and information. Without that he would be lost. "On your own terms, then. But I want to know what happened to him. I want an explanation I can accept."

"You'll have the truth!" George said. "I won't concoct an explanation just to satisfy you. If I can't find out how he came to fall, you'll have to accept it."

Franks nodded, but the idea of a continuing mystery seemed to terrify him.

"What will you do?"

"You'll have to leave that to me," George said. It would hardly inspire confidence if he admitted he had no idea.

Muriel, who had been curled up like a child in the corner of the sofa, her dressing gown wrapped around her bare feet, watching them in a daze of grief, suddenly stirred.

"I wish there was something I could do," she said. "It's the waiting for news that's so hard . . ."

George felt she still had not grasped what had happened. He thought some well-meaning doctor had given her a sedative, and her mind wandered between dream and reality. It was as if she believed Greg might walk in through the door any moment.

"You could talk to me about Greg," he said. "That would help."

"What good would that do!" Franks said. "I'm not paying you to sit on your arse in our front room. The police have been here all morning with their questions."

George ignored him. "Did the police ask you about drugs?" he asked her.

The woman nodded. "I told them Greg was a good boy," she said. "He'd never do anything like that."

"Did Greg ever have visitors here?" George asked.

"No," she said. "When he was living here, I told him to

bring his friends home more. I would have liked to meet them. But he never did.''

"What about phone calls?'' George's voice was soft and coaxing. "Were there any of those?''

"Oh,'' she said, and she almost laughed. "There were always phone calls. You know what it's like with birdwatching. Wanting to know what was about and where to go. Even when he had left home, they still phoned here.''

"Did you take messages for him?''

"Sometimes,'' she said. "Not often. I don't think they trusted me. If Greg wasn't in, they said they'd phone back.''

"Did you get any names?'' George asked. "Did he have any special friends?''

She was a lonely woman, he thought. She had no life of her own. It was possible that she had lived vicariously through Greg, cherishing his friends as her own, taking an interest in all their activities.

"They didn't talk to me,'' she said sadly. "Not really. Just asked for Greg when I answered the phone. Sometimes I asked him about them, and he'd tell me. There was a Mr. Pym who used to phone sometimes. He was a nicely spoken gentleman. Greg said he was a teacher at the high school on the heath. 'You want to keep in with him,' I told Greg. 'That's the class of friend you need.' ''

"And did Greg keep in with Roger Pym?'' George asked.

"I don't know,'' she said. "Not lately. When Greg was a lad, before he could drive, I think Mr. Pym took them out birdwatching at the weekends a couple of times. To the reservoirs. Chew Valley Lake. You know.''

"Them?'' George asked. "Who else went on these trips, Mrs. Franks?''

She shrugged. She did not know. Lads from school, she supposed. Greg had always been one for keeping himself to himself.

George thought Greg must have been keeping his private life secret for years if the only name she could remember was of a man who had taken her son birdwatching when he was still a schoolboy.

"Did Greg have a girlfriend?'' George asked.

95

Her eyes filled again with tears. The reality of Greg's death had overwhelmed her once more. She was realising that there would be no wedding, no daughter-in-law, no grandchildren.

"He went out sometimes with girls," she said. "I heard him talking to them sometimes on the phone, arranging to pick them up. I saw him with one in town last year, just after Christmas. It was Saturday afternoon, and I'd been to the winter sales. He didn't see me. She was a real beauty. Tall and blond, like something you'd see on the front of a magazine. And the clothes she wore! He never brought her home. I expect he was ashamed of us."

Dennis Franks had been standing by the window with his back to the room during the conversation. Now he turned around and glared at George.

"What do you think you're doing with all these questions?" he said. "This won't do any good. You know who was on the boat with you. You should be talking to them, not to us."

"I'll be doing that, too," George said. He allowed Mrs. Franks to shrink back into the comfort of the sofa and directed the next question to her husband. "Your son always had a lot of money," he said. "Didn't it occur to you to wonder how a young man could have achieved such an income?"

"I thought he was doing well for himself," Franks said proudly. "A chip off the old block, I thought. A businessman. I built my company up from nothing, too."

"How did you think he made his money?"

"Buying and selling, he said when I asked him."

"You must have realised it was likely that he was involved in something illegal."

"I didn't know that," Franks said defensively. "So maybe it was all pound notes, I thought. Maybe he's not telling the taxman everything. We all do a bit of that, don't we? I broke a few rules when I started out. Still do, probably, but I've got a good accountant."

George would have said, rather pompously, that he considered tax evasion as much a crime as theft or burglary, but

Franks was continuing, "Besides, I'd not seen the boy for months. I don't know what he'd been up to recently."

There was a silence. A lone bus rumbled past the window. George was reminded of his last visit to the house, when he had been tempted by the prospect of Cornish seabirds to sacrifice his judgement and reason. The result had been a new seabird for the world and a murder. He had not needed Dennis Franks to tell him that he had responsibility in the case.

He knew that they were waiting for him to go. Muriel Franks had withdrawn into daydreams and memories, and Dennis shuffled and looked at his watch.

"There's just one more question before I go," George said.

They both stared at him.

"You knew where Greg would be this weekend because you opened a letter sent to him here," George said. He tried to sound as if this were a normal thing to do. If Muriel Franks thought he was accusing her of prying, she might lie. "Had that ever happened before?"

She was suddenly hysterical, transferred from her sedated lethargy. Tears streamed down her cheeks, and her voice was loud and frightened. "I didn't know what was in it!" she cried. "He had no right to be angry. It was no reason for him to leave home."

George looked for explanation to Dennis Franks.

"We should have told you before," the man said. He looked embarrassed, not by the revelation that his wife had opened Greg's mail but by the scene she was making now. "That's when he left home for good. It was about a year ago. He said if he couldn't trust Muriel not to interfere in his private life, he'd have to go." George moved from his seat to the sofa where Mrs. Franks was sobbing. He wished Molly had agreed to come with him.

"What was in the letter you opened?" he asked, not sure how to speak to her without provoking another outburst of guilt and self-pity.

She looked at him wide-eyed, gasping in an attempt to stop the crying.

97

"It was a cheque," she said, "for a lot of money."

George showed no surprise. "Was there a letter with the cheque?"

"No," she said. "Not really a letter. One of those printed slips."

"A compliment slip," Franks said impatiently. "She means a compliment slip."

"Was there a name?" George asked. "Can you remember?"

She shook her head. "Something was written on it in ordinary handwriting," she said. She wanted to please him. "I can't remember what it said."

"Are you sure?" he asked. "Perhaps you could try."

She shook her head. "It was just one line," she said. "A scribble." Then, glad because at least she had some information, she added. "There was an address printed at the top of the paper. I recognized it because we've been there before. Not to the house, of course. We wouldn't know anyone who lived in a place like that. But to the pub in the village. Den used to take me out for a drive in the evening if it was sunny, and we'd have steak and chips in the garden. . . ."

The aimless words rambled on. George interrupted, trying not to show his impatience. "Mrs. Franks," he said, "what was the address?"

She looked at him in surprise, as if she thought she had already told him.

"It was in Pemberton," she said calmly. "It's a pretty village in Somerset. The house was called Cranmers. It's right in the middle of the village, and we drive past it on the way to the pub." Then, politely, as if making conversation to one of her husband's business friends, she said, "Do you know Pemberton, Mr. Palmer-Jones?"

George said nothing, but he knew the village. He and a friend had been invited there after an education and wildlife conference to share a meal with another of the conference members. He remembered the house because of the unusual name. The friend was Gwen Pullen, the curator of the Natural History Museum, and the man who had offered them hospitality was Duncan James.

George thought Anne James looked like the heroine of a Betjeman poem. She was long-legged, healthy, and very English. He could imagine her on the tennis courts. She would play a stylish but unshowy game, and she would not try too hard to win. He arrived at Cranmers with no clear idea what he would say to her, and when he saw her across the perfect lawn, he felt intimidated by her middle-class competence.

It was midafternoon. He had parked in the middle of the village and walked back to the house, passing the pub where the Franks ate steak and chips on the momentous days when Dennis took out his wife. Pemberton was surrounded by low, rich agricultural land with fields which flooded in winter.

There were black-and-white cows and black-and-white houses, and everywhere fruit trees. Cranmers was made of flat-faced stone, and it was square and more regularly proportioned than the other houses in the street. It had three storeys, and on one side there was a glass-and-wrought-iron verandah. A Virginia creeper which was just starting to change colour was climbing over one corner. The house was protected from the road by a stone wall and wrought iron gate.

He could tell while he was still on the pavement that a children's party was taking place in the garden. He heard the tuneless singing of "Happy Birthday" interspersed with giggles over the wall, and the gate was festooned with coloured balloons. By the time he had opened the gate, the tea was over. A trestle table with benches on each side had been set on the lawn, but the children had run away into the orchard and were climbing trees and pushing each other on a tyre strung by a piece of rope from an apple tree. The elaborate homemade birthday cake was still uncut.

Anne James approached him over the grass. She was wearing a sleeveless floral dress and sandals, and the courteous friendliness that comes with supreme confidence.

"Have you come to collect one of the little monsters?" she asked. "I don't think I'll be able to persuade them to leave yet."

"No," he said. "It's not that."

99

She looked at him then more closely. Before, her attention had been on the brown-limbed children in the orchard, checking their safety, enjoying the fun.

"I've met you before, haven't I?" she said. "It's Mr. Palmer-Jones."

"Yes." He was not surprised that she had remembered him. She had been an attentive hostess. She would do everything well. "I worked occasionally with your husband."

"Duncan isn't here," she said. "He says he's sorry to be away for Philip's birthday, but I think he's rather glad. He finds the chaos a little daunting. He's in Cornwall, and he couldn't have come home even if he'd wanted to. There was some sort of accident, apparently, and the police have asked him to stay."

"I know," George said. "That's why I'm here."

"Oh," she said vaguely. "Don't you work for the police? I remembered Duncan's saying." She looked at him anxiously, too polite to say that George looked too old to be a policeman.

"No," George said. "Not the police. The Home Office."

"So you're involved with the investigation into the accident?"

He did not answer directly. "It wasn't an accident," he said. "It was murder."

"I don't understand," she said. "Duncan is all right?" Yet, even in her anxiety, she maintained her composure.

"Yes," he said, "Duncan is fine. But I should like to ask you some questions. The police will be coming to talk to you, too. I'm not here in any official capacity. There's no reason why you should talk to me, but I've been asked by the parents of the boy who died to look into his death. They feel the police in Cornwall are a bit remote. I was on the boat, you see."

"But why are you here? I can't help you."

He shrugged. "I had to come to Bristol to see Mr. and Mrs. Franks, and this is on the way back to Porthkennan."

Parents began to arrive then to collect the children. George stood beside Anne James as she cut the cake and wrapped it in kitchen paper. She handed it out to them with little presents in silver paper decorated with ribbon. The adults gathered sticky and excitable children to them and drove off in expensive cars. When the lawn was empty and Lucy and Philip, shouting the last impatient goodbyes, had been released back to the orchard, Anne led him to a white garden bench in the shadow of a yew hedge.

"Is Duncan in some sort of trouble?" she asked. She was more intelligent than he had realised.

"I don't know," he said. It was hard to imagine Duncan James, upright and respectable, in trouble of any kind.

"There must be something," she said, "or you'd not have come here."

It was five o'clock, and in the long shadow it was pleasantly cool after the heat of the day. Somewhere in the village there was a bonfire.

"Did he ever talk to you about Greg Franks?" George asked.

She shook her head. "Is that the boy who died?"

"Yes."

"No," she said. "I've never heard of him."

"He's a birdwatcher," George said. "A twitcher. He's quite famous in his own circles. The police believe he was bringing drugs into the country."

"Duncan would never be involved in anything like that."

"No," George said. "I don't believe he would. Unfortunately there is a connection between Duncan and Franks. About a year ago a letter arrived at Greg's parents' house. He was still officially living at home then, though he would disappear for days, even weeks, at a time. The letter arrived during one of his frequent absences, and his mother opened it. It was a large cheque, and it was sent from this address. You say you've never heard of Greg, so presumably you didn't send it. That leaves Duncan."

She shook her head. "There must be some mistake," she said. "I don't know anything about it."

"You do see how it looks," George persisted. "Franks was a known drug dealer. Duncan paid him a large sum of money. That implicates Duncan in the drugs, don't you see?"

"I can see how it looks," she said, "but it's impossible."

101

"You can think of no other reason Duncan might have had for paying Franks?"

"No," she said. "None at all."

He found it impossible to follow the line of questioning, and there was a pause in the conversation. In the tall trees behind the house he heard wood pigeons calling, and in the garden behind the wall there was the sound of a hose.

"Why did Duncan go to Cornwall this weekend?" George asked at last.

"He was tired," Anne said. "He needed the break."

"I shouldn't have thought it was his sort of thing at all. When did he decide to go?"

"Last weekend," she said. "It was all rather sudden. I was pleased; I thought he could do with a holiday. There's a lot of pressure on the sites of scientific interest in the area, and he's been under strain for months."

"How did he come to hear of the trip?"

"I don't know exactly," she said. "I presume it was some sort of circular. A letter came for him on Saturday morning, and later that day at dinner he said something like 'This looks interesting. Would you mind if I went?' "

"Did you read the circular?"

"No," she said. "But if you want to see it, I expect it's still in Duncan's office. He never throws anything away."

She stood up and, with a last look at the children, led him into the house. He thought it was her confidence which made her so trusting. She was so secure that she believed this relative stranger could do her family no harm. Inside it was cool, ordered, cared for, without being uncomfortably tidy. Children's Wellingtons stood in a row just inside the door. Anne must have been picking apples, because there was a box of them, wrapped separately in newspaper, in the hall. Duncan's study was a mess of papers and files. An open ordnance survey map was spread over the floor, and they had to step over it to get to the desk. On the desk a rack of plastic trays was spilling over with letters. "It'll be here somewhere," she said, working through the papers in the top tray. "It's doesn't look like it, but there's a kind of system." He watched her pile letters and bills into some kind of order.

"Here we are," she said. "This is the telephone bill. It came on Saturday, too."

"What's that?" George said, pointing to a printed white envelope.

She opened it and pulled out a glossy brochure.

"No," she said. "This is an advertisement for a new leisure complex in the county. There's been controversy over it for years, since the original plans were proposed. It's in the middle of Rashwood Park. Duncan supervised the environmental impact assessment. There was a lot of opposition to the project locally, but unfortunately he couldn't find any habitat rare or important enough to stop it going ahead."

"Could I have a look?" George asked.

The development company was called Squirrel, and the publicity was emblazoned with a logo of oak leaves and acorns. The complex included a four-star hotel and golf course, a health club and gymnasium. It had been open for six months, and the photographs showed scrawny middle-aged women drinking cocktails by a swimming pool. On the border of the front page, in red ink, was written a Bristol phone number.

"Did this arrive on Saturday?" George asked.

"Yes," Anne said vaguely. "It must have. It was next to the telephone bill."

"Did you see Duncan open the circular about the *Jessie Ellen* trip?"

"No," she said, "I don't think I did. Lucy goes to ballet on Saturday morning, and I was in a hurry."

"Would you mind if I kept this?" he asked, holding out the glossy booklet.

"No," she said. "Keep it." Saunas and jacuzzis would not appeal to her, he thought. She would think them common.

They stood, suddenly awkward, in the little room. He was challenging the confidence which had seen her through so far. She was starting to realise he might be dangerous. She felt George had betrayed her. She had thought he was one of her sort. Now here they were together, rifling through the private papers on her husband's desk.

"Look," she said, "I don't like this. Perhaps I shouldn't have talked to you. Duncan's done nothing wrong, but I think I should have spoken to him first. You'd better go."

Somewhere in the house, a long way off, a child was wailing that it was hungry.

"Yes," George said. "I'll leave now. I'm sorry to have put you in a difficult position."

She ignored the complaining child and walked with him to the front door and waited there until she was sure he had left the garden.

He walked back down the street to his car. A group of loud-voiced young people were sitting on the grass in the pub's garden. At the car he paused. He looked again at the glossy brochure advertising the delights of Rashwood Hall Country Club. On an impulse he crossed the road to the public telephone box, feeling in his pocket for change as he went. He dialed the number written by hand on the brochure.

The phone was answered by a young woman with a West Country accent.

"Yes," she said.

"Is Greg in?" George asked, his fingers were crossed behind his back.

"No," she said. "He's away this week."

She was bright and chatty. She wasn't the sort to read the newspaper or listen to the news, he thought. She didn't even know Greg was dead.

"When are you expecting him back?" He tried to sound friendly, not really interested but enjoying a conversation with a young woman.

"Well," she said, "you know what Greg's like. The end of the week, he said."

"He wanted some information," George said. "Perhaps I'd better post it to him. Could you give me the address?"

She seemed suddenly different, not suspicious, but careful, like a child who has been warned not to give too much away. "I think it might be best if you phoned again when he's back," she said.

"I'm in Bristol tonight," he said, jovial, fatherly. "Perhaps I could drop it in."

"I'm sorry," she said, meaning it but pleased, too, that she had an excuse for putting him off. "There won't be anyone here. I'm just on my way to work."

"That's a shame," he said, "having to work on a lovely evening like this."

"Well, it's not really work. Pleasure, really. I'm personal assistant to Brian Barnes of Squirrel Development. We're entertaining some clients at Rashwood Hall."

She giggled smugly. George wished her a pleasant evening and said he hoped Mr. Barnes appreciated her, then replaced the receiver. He went back over the road, then to the pub for a drink. He told himself that it was because he needed change for the other phone calls he still had to make, but it was more like a celebration.

9

When George approached the entrance to the Squirrel leisure complex, he realised he had been to Rashwood Park once before. His son had been a student at Bristol University, and he and Molly had come to know the city well during his time there. They had visited Rashwood Park when they spent a weekend with him before taking him home for the summer vacation. There had been an end-of-term party, a picnic lunch, and George and Molly had been invited. It had all been rather posey and pretentious—there were girls wearing Victorian underwear, with flowers in their hair, and young men with loud voices discussing art. Molly had hated it and muttered throughout the festivity about privilege and decadence. He had found it amusing. Both had agreed that the setting for the picnic was spectacular and had encouraged extravagant posturing.

They had driven out of the city and down the narrow country roads to the grounds of a ruined Georgian mansion which were apparently open to the public. It was a magnificent lush crumbling place with ivy-covered pillars, the empty stone bowls of giant fountains, and broken statues overgrown with honeysuckle and convolvulus. Below the houses there had been a lake with flag iris at its edge and a forest of bramble and beech beyond, and on the low ground between the lake and the house a meadow of wildflowers and long grasses. George seemed to remember that they all drank too much wine, and one of the nymphlike girls spoilt the image of purity by being sick.

Now everything was quite different. The old mansion had been demolished. Nothing was left of the pillars and towering arches, though there were mean little arches in brick leading from the bar of the new hotel to a patio of bright pink stone. And there, in a corner, cleaned and scrubbed, was one of the statues from the old garden. The grass was nitrate-green and was being mowed again—quite unnecessarily it seemed to George—by a man sitting on a noisy machine.

The developer had retained the lake, but now it had concrete sides to allow easy access for the wind surfers, and it was surrounded by a complex of self-catering houses which varied in architectural style from Mediterranean villas to Swiss chalets. The meadow had been drained to form part of the golf course.

When George made a phone call from Pemberton to Gwen Pullen, the curator of the museum, to ask her to dinner at Rashwood Park, she had been horrified.

"What do you want to stay there for?" she demanded. "It's a hideous place, George. And the food will be disgusting. Besides, its immoral to support the scheme. It'll only encourage the developer to do the same thing somewhere else."

Now at the lodge which still marked the entrance to the estate, George thought she had been right. He could not stay in the place and put money into the pockets of the developer who had caused such desecration. Even while he was working on an investigation, he would not do it. Much better to sleep in the car somewhere and find another way to meet Greg Frank's girlfriend. But even as he hesitated, he knew these were moral scruples he could not afford. This place had some relevance in the relationship between Duncan James and Greg Franks. Besides, he had managed to persuade Gwen to come to Rashwood Park to eat with him, and she knew more about seabirds than anyone else in Britain. He drove up the pink gravel drive and parked in front of the hotel.

He had worried when he had booked the night at Rashwood Park that they would not allow him into the dining room in such casual clothes, or that at least his attire would make him conspicuous, but his anxiety was unfounded. It was not that sort of hotel. The guests seemed rather to pride themselves on their informality. They sat in the bar in track-suits, with towels round their necks, and talked about hand-icaps and forehands and weights. It was much worse, George thought, than pretentious young men talking about art. Even Molly would concede that.

The receptionist behind a pine desk in the entrance hall wore an orange jumpsuit. All the staff, it seemed, wore orange uniforms.

"I telephoned earlier," he said when at last he caught her attention, "and booked a room for tonight."

She nodded distantly, so he thought at first she still had not heard him, but when she gave him his key, she smiled a toothy and unnatural leer—as much part of the corporate design, George thought, as the uniform, and for one dreadful minute he was afraid she would tell him to "have a nice day." His bedroom had a colour television, miniature bar, and shower, none of which he wanted. He would have pre-ferred a real bath and a pile of thick warm towels. The bed had a duvet—an import from the Continent which he de-tested. Already suitably angry, he went downstairs to meet Gwen Pullen and to find Greg Franks' girlfriend and the Mr. Barnes who was responsible for such a monstrous building.

Gwen Pullen was sitting in the bar, drinking whisky, wait-ing for him. She was a middle-aged spinster, large-boned, a little clumsy, and shyness sometimes made her loud and hearty. She waved a large black handbag at him to attract his attention, and he wondered if it had been a mistake to ask her to come. He had hoped to sit, quiet and unnoticed, until he heard the voice he recognised as belonging to the girl he had telephoned earlier. Gwen, with her untidy shock of black hair and her dark-rimmed spectacles, being jolly and girlish, was hard to hide. He bought a drink and sat beside her.

"George," she said. "My dear, how's Molly? I've had Roger Pym on the telephone to me all day."

"Were you able to help him?"

108

"I'm not sure," she said. "Not with a skin. I've checked everything we have at the museum, and there's nothing at all that fits the description of the bird you saw. Then I remembered seeing something in the journal of a rather tedious and unadventurous nineteenth-century explorer that came into my possession a couple of years ago. He led an expedition to the Aleutian Islands and recorded a colony of petrels extremely similar to the bird you saw."

"With red feet?" George interrupted.

"Yes," she said. "Very definitely with red feet. He didn't take any specimens—not because he was squeamish but because, I gather, he was a very poor shot. I don't know of any more recent expeditions to the Aleutians—there's nothing in the literature. The Island he mentioned is uninhabited and quite hard to get to. But it might be worth a visit. Roger Pym is already making plans, I think."

"Yes," George said, "he would be."

"I understand he found the bird," Gwen said, "so I can understand why he's excited. He's already thinking of names, you know. Pym's petrel sounds a bit pretentious, don't you think?" George said nothing.

He stood up and led her towards the dining room. It was possible Franks' mysterious girlfriend and her boss were already there. He chose a table at the far side of the room, so he had a view of the whole restaurant and anybody coming in or out. He sat Gwen with her face to the wall, hoping to make her slightly less conspicuous.

"What are you doing here anyway, George?" she asked. "Is it just about the bird? It wouldn't have anything to do with Greg Franks, would it?"

"Did you know him?" George asked, surprised, in a low voice, hoping she would match the volume of hers to his.

"He came into the museum occasionally before his trips to exotic places, trying to get information about the birds he might see there. He could be an awful nuisance, but I rather liked him." She looked around her and said, "Whatever possessed you to stay in a dreadful place like this? You'd be more comfortable on the sofa in my flat."

He shrugged and waited until the waiter had deposited tepid soup in front of them.

"It might have a bearing on Greg Franks' death," he said. "How on earth did they get planning permission?"

"George," she said roguishly, "I do believe you're changing the subject."

"No," he said. "Really. It might be important."

"We're all supposed to be attracting tourism," she said. "The service industry, I believe they call it. It's the same at the museum. There's no money for any real research anymore. No money for paying reputable biologists. The whole place is staffed now by starving young graduates on some government scheme. They're very pleasant children, and they try their best, but as soon as we've trained them up, they come to the end of their contract and have to move on. Yet we do seem to have money for a new restaurant, where the food is actually almost as disgusting as in here, and we do seem to have money to renovate the shop so we can sell toy dinosaurs and lousy tea towels. That apparently is what the public wants, so that's the service we have to provide."

He waited until she had run out of breath. He knew better than to stop her in midflow.

"So the council bent the planning rules because they think Rashwood Park will attract tourists?" he said.

"No," she said. "No, I don't actually think any rules were bent. Rashwood isn't in the greenbelt. It isn't a site of special scientific interest. Some of the botanists at the museum were muttering that it should have been. They claimed some rare plant or other. But there was no evidence. It was all anecdotal. And when Duncan James came to do his survey, he didn't find anything, so there were no grounds to prevent the planning application's going ahead."

"I only came here once before it was ruined," he said, "but I thought the woodland looked very good, and that the lake might attract some wildfowl. Didn't any of the local birdwatchers come here? They might have found something to give it the status of a site of special scientific interest."

"The only person I knew to cover it all," she said, "was

your friend Greg Franks. And that was a long time ago. Before he started this twitching business."

As soon as the meal was over, she said she had to go. Some of the children in her department were coming round to her flat for a talk, she said, about their futures. They were really very good, and there were still some institutions in the country not seduced by the notion of the service industry. She hoped she might be able to help them.

He lingered in the restaurant over the coffee and recognised the voice of the young woman who had spoken to him on the phone as soon as she entered the restaurant. The place was quite quiet. As she walked through the swinging doors, she was laughing. It was good-humoured, innocent laughter. Her head was thrown back, and her mouth was open. She could still not have heard, George thought, that Greg was dead. She was almost certainly the woman Mrs. Franks had seen with her son, shopping in Bristol. She was blond, beautiful, and long-legged. Her clothes were obviously expensive. Yet she made no attempt at sophistication. These good times were a novelty to her; she knew enough about the world to think they would not last. She intended to enjoy every moment of them while she had the chance.

There were four of them, and they sat at the best table in the restaurant, by a window with a view down the garden to the lake. The woman's companion, whom George took to be Barnes, was a square fat man built like a bull terrier. He seemed to say very little but ate with a ravenous intensity, as if he had known great hunger. They were entertaining another couple, who ate little but drank heavily throughout the meal. As the evening progressed, the couple, who were middle-aged, conventionally dressed, became more and more wrapped up in each other, sharing their own bottle of wine, their own domestic jokes, so Barnes and Franks' girlfriend might have been strangers placed at the table by chance.

George called for more coffee and waited, listening as best he could, to what was being said at the table some distance from him. Once he looked up and caught Barnes' eye. He wondered if he had caused the man to be suspicious of him, but that seemed ridiculous. Then he began to fear that it

111

would be impossible for him to talk to the young woman on her own. He imagined them in some private room, drinking together until late that night or sweeping down the drive in one of the ostentatious cars parked outside. In the end Barnes made it easy for him. While she was still eating dessert, he pulled a twenty-pound note from his pocket and passed it across the table to her.

"Gus and I have some business to discuss," he said. "Get yourself a taxi home. I'll see you in the office tomorrow."

He stomped through the dining room on his short, fat legs, aware that all the waitresses knew he was the boss and were staring at him, followed by the middle-aged couple, who walked like grotesque bridesmaids, a couple of paces behind him.

Greg's girlfriend seemed unoffended by her dismissal. She sat for a moment scraping the last remnants of chocolate sauce from her pudding bowl and looking out the window. It was dark, and coloured spotlights lit up the trees by the lake and the statue on the patio outside. She gathered up her handbag, and waving cheerfully to the waitresses, she wandered out to the bar. Her hair was very long and tied up in an elaborate plait. George followed her. He expected her to go immediately to one of the public phones in reception to call a taxi, but she stopped instead at the bar and perched on one of the tall stools, her smooth legs crossed. The barman obviously knew and liked her, and there was a lot of good-humoured banter. Again George felt unable to approach her, and he sat waiting until she was on her own. Suddenly the bar was busier. A group of middle-aged men came in demanding drinks all at once. Conversation with the barman was impossible, and she slipped from the stool and wandered into a quiet corner. George went up to her.

"I'm sorry to disturb you," he said. "I wanted to talk to you about Greg Franks."

She looked up without suspicion, smiling. "You phoned me this evening." she said. "I was getting ready to come out."

He nodded.

"Sit down," she said easily. Perhaps she thought he was
112

too old to do her any harm. Perhaps she thought she could look after herself.

"I'm sorry," he said. "I've some very bad news."

"About Greg?"

He nodded again.

"Has he been arrested?"

"No," George said. "Would that be likely?"

She shrugged and, for the first time, regarded him with suspicion.

"Are you the police?"

"No," he said, and she smiled at him. She had an artificial tan and a big friendly smile that was completely different from the receptionist's. Her teeth were very white in the brown face.

"I was in Cornwall with Greg," George said. "We were on a boat, birdwatching. I'm afraid he's dead."

"No," she said, wanting to think it was a mistake, a joke in bad taste, but held by his age and authority. "I don't believe it. Why haven't I heard?"

"It was on the radio," George said gently. "The police informed his parents. I suppose they didn't know to come to you."

"He was so well," she cried. "Was it an accident?"

"He was drowned," George said. "The police think it was murder."

Then she began to cry. There was little shock in the tears. She was not surprised by disaster. She spent her life expecting it. Her happiness had always been precarious.

In the bar the businessmen were becoming rowdy. There was boozy laughter and loud, crude jokes.

"Let me take you home," George said. "We can't talk here."

"I don't know you," she said, but it was almost a formality. She was not really frightened of him.

"I'm a friend of Greg's," he said, and she looked at him gratefully because that allowed her to trust him.

"Greg never wanted anyone to know where he was living," she said. "But I don't suppose it matters now."

She directed him back to the city and along the river to a

113

hilly district below the suspension bridge, with narrow winding streets and terraced houses. Obviously it had become fashionable since George had known the area well. There was a new delicatessen on one corner, and on another an old lady stood bewildered on the pavement staring into a dimly lit wine bar where once her local pub must have been. Ferndale Avenue was wider than most of the streets and backed onto a churchyard. The houses were Edwardian, big, and had been divided into flats. They would be too expensive for students and most single young people, and George thought the population would be elderly, shabby, respectable. Occasionally they passed an uncurtained window, and George saw elegant, decaying rooms, a piano, a canary in a large hanging cage.

"It's number seven," she said. "You can park round the corner in the alley."

Discretion had become a habit, he thought. Greg would not want the neighbours to see how many visitors came to the house. He followed her instructions. In the dark lane behind the house she got out of the car, smoothing her skirt automatically, searching in her bag for her keys.

"I'm sorry," he said. "I don't even know your name."

"Didn't Greg talk about me, then?"

"Not to me," George said. "Perhaps to the others, who were younger." But she seemed not to believe him.

"It's Vicky," she said. "Vicky Jones."

The night was hot and humid. There was the smell of dusty streets and the trees in the churchyard. She used one key to let them into a cool gloomy hall painted with green gloss paint and a second to open the door to her ground-floor flat. She switched on a light and drew the curtains. That was a habit, too, George thought, a ritual.

The room was big and square. It was conventionally furnished—at one end was a glass dining room table and four chairs and at the other a sofa which might have been bought at any High Street store. But there were touches of excess: a cream leather chair, a very expensive hi-fi system, and in one corner a stuffed and mounted gazelle. Vicky saw George looking at the animal.

114

"Greg bought it," she said. "It was a present. After one of his trips abroad."

"How long had you been living together?" George asked.

"About a year," she said. "On and off. He went away a lot. On business."

"What business was that?"

She shrugged. "He'd never tell me," she said. "And in the end I thought it better not to ask."

"But you guessed?"

"I suppose so."

"Didn't it make any difference to you?" George asked. "The fact that Greg was a drug dealer?"

She looked at him, wondering if he would understand if she explained. Perhaps she decided he was too old. "Look," she said. "He was fun. At first that was enough."

Yes, George thought. It was true. Greg had been fun. He said nothing, and she took his silence as condemnation.

"You can't understand what it was like!" she said. "I've been in care since I was six. First I was in a children's home, like a workhouse, run by a bunch of nuns. Then they moved me to a foster family. They were all right, kind enough, but kids moved through that house like peas on a conveyor belt. Short-term care, they called it, and they were only used to giving short-term love. I got left there for some reason, and the love ran out. When I was sixteen, I was out on my own, and since then no one's given a monkey's what happened to me. I felt I'd missed out on everything. I wanted a good time, colour, music, excitement. Two years ago I met Greg. He made me feel so special. You don't know. He'd send me flowers. Bring me presents. Take me out dancing all night. Then he'd disappear, sometimes for weeks. It was birdwatching, he'd say. It was always birdwatching."

"He really was a birdwatcher," George said.

"I know." And for the first time since he had told her of Greg's death, she smiled. "Sometimes I went out with him. It was such fun. Everyone seemed to know him. I went to Porthkennan once and stayed at Myrtle Cottage."

"But you thought that sometimes he used birdwatching as an excuse?"

She nodded. "At first I thought he was going away with other women. Perhaps he was. I wouldn't have minded. As long as he came back to me. And he always did. Then sometimes he would have so much money. Hundreds, thousands of pounds, all in cash. When I asked what he did, he said he was an entrepreneur. He bought and sold, he said. Whatever people wanted."

"When did you start work for Mr. Barnes?"

The sudden change of question did not appear to surprise her. Shock had made her passive, responsive. She would be afraid of taking the initiative. Besides, she was used to doing as she was told.

"About three years ago. I took a typing course straight after school; then I went to work in his office. Just as a junior at first, typing and filing. I became his personal assistant six months ago."

"What does that involve?"

Again she smiled and answered the unspoken question. "Nothing smutty," she said. "Nothing like that. Sometimes he likes me to go to dinner with him and his clients. That's all. He never married. In the office I'm more like a personal secretary."

"Did Greg ever ask you about your work?" George asked.

Her mood changed suddenly, and she looked uncertain and resentful. "Who *are* you?" she demanded. "Why are you asking all these questions? You must be a policeman."

"No," he said. "I promise I'm not a policeman. I've been asked by Greg's parents to find out why he died and who killed him."

She accepted his explanation immediately and looked up at him with fresh tears. "He never got on with his parents. He said they crowded him. I told him he was lucky to have a mum and dad who bothered about him."

"You can understand why they're so upset," George said, playing on her sentiment. "They loved Greg as much as you did."

"Yes," she said. "It must be dreadful for them."

"Greg did talk to you about your work, didn't he?" George

116

asked gently. "Especially about the Rashwood Park complex?"

"He said he couldn't understand how they came to get planning permission to build on the site," she said. "He used to go birdwatching in the park, and he said the lake was brilliant in the winter." She looked up apologetically. "He told me what birds he'd seen there," she said, "but I never could remember their names. I think it made him cross because I couldn't get more interested."

"So he was surprised when Squirrel developed Rashwood Park?" George said, prompting her, trying to bring her back to the subject, wishing he had Molly's patience for this sort of interview.

"There were flowers, too," she said. "Rare flowers."

"Did he ask you to try to find out how the company gained planning permission?" George asked.

She nodded. "At first he thought Mr. Barnes must have bribed some of the councillors on the planning committee," she said, "but I brought home a report from the Nature Conservancy Council which said that there were no rare species in the site, and there was no reason to give it special protection."

So then George knew how Greg Franks and Duncan James were connected. Barnes had not bribed the councillors on Somerset's planning committees, but the apparently incorruptible regional officer of the Nature Conservancy Council had. Greg had found out and had blackmailed Duncan James. The cheque in the letter Mrs. Franks had opened was one payment. The Rashwood brochure sent to Cranmers was an indication that another was required. Presumably Duncan had phoned the number on the brochure and had been summoned to Cornwall.

Vicky got up and disappeared into a bedroom. When she returned, her face had been washed and more makeup applied.

"Did Greg tell you what he intended to do with the information you'd given him?" George asked. "Was he planning to go to the police?"

"Oh, no," she said. "Nothing like that." She looked at

117

him, a little embarrassed. "He said it would be a nice little earner. The import business was getting a bit risky, he said. He'd have to start taking more care. The new line might be more profitable. He seemed pleased with me. Soon afterwards he moved into the flat full-time."

"Did Greg tell you anything about this weekend in Cornwall?" George asked. "It might help me find out who killed him."

"He was looking forward to it," she said. "He told me it would be a real laugh. 'A boat full of people who either hate me or owe me money, or both, all having to be polite,' he said." She looked awkwardly at George again. "That makes him sound horrible," she said, "but really he wasn't. He was so clever at describing people. He would have come home at the end of the week and told me stories about them, so I would have laughed and laughed."

"Did he tell you any stories about them before he went?" George asked.

She shook her head.

"Did he tell you who was going to be there?"

"No, he didn't tell me anything else about it at all. But I knew he was looking forward to it."

George imagined Greg's planning the weekend with a sort of gleeful mischief. Who else, he wondered, was Greg blackmailing? Who hated him and why? He tried to remember the night and day on the *Jessie Ellen*. There was tension, but all the details had disappeared in the elation after the petrel.

"Did Mr. Barnes know that Greg was blackmailing Duncan James about the conservation report?" George asked.

"I didn't say anything about blackmail!" She felt she had betrayed Greg with her confidence.

"But that's what he meant," George said seriously. "Isn't it?"

"I don't know," she said. "I suppose so."

Greg had made her happy, so she had persuaded herself he was beyond morality, manipulating people for his own amusement. And to entertain her.

118

"Did Mr. Barnes know what was going on?" George asked.

"No. Of course not. He's a dangerous man. He wouldn't allow anything to threaten his business."

"But Greg was threatening it," George said. "Duncan James might have decided that he couldn't take any more pressure and gone to the authorities."

"I don't know if Greg ever thought about that," she said.

"What would Barnes have done if he'd found out?"

"I don't know," she said again.

Perhaps Barnes *had* found out, George thought. Perhaps one of the *Jessie Ellen*'s passengers had been paid by him to murder Greg. Then he thought he was being silly. Barnes was a businessman, not a gangster, and the idea that one of the people staying at Myrtle Cottage was a professional killer was laughable.

Vicky was lost in thought, and he decided it was time to go.

"Look," he said, "can I get in touch with anyone to stay the night with you? A friend or a relative?"

But he knew the answer before she replied. "No," she said. "There's no one."

He was in the gloomy hall when she called him back.

"People didn't realise," she said. "With Greg it was a game, a bluff. He didn't do it for the money. Not really. It was the excitement, the sense of power. If the people hadn't paid him, he would never have used the information he had against them. That's not blackmail. Is it?"

But she didn't wait for an answer, and with her image of Greg reconstructed, she returned to her flat.

George stood for a moment, collecting his thoughts under a streetlight. The street was quiet. He realised later that the car must have been parked with others outside the flats. He did not hear the noise of the engine until he had turned up the alley, and then it was so close behind him and the head-lamps were so bright that there was little he could do to escape. He squeezed against the high brick wall just in time, and he thought it was a drunken driver, that he had had a close shave. It was only when the car braked sharply and backed with a sudden screech of tyres, then came at him again, that he realised he was the target of a deliberate attack. There was nothing then that he could do. The bonnet of the car caught him and threw him towards a row of dustbins stacked neatly against a wall. Just before he lost consciousness, he heard the clatter of a lid as it fell onto the alley and saw the trail light of the car as it disappeared into the main street.

10

When Claire Bingham had finished the interviews with the guests at Myrtle Cottage, Wargan called her back to Heanor and told her the investigation lacked direction. He had been speaking to an officer from the serious crime squad in Bristol about Rosco's previous conviction for arson. It was, it seemed, a simple act of revenge. He had been sacked from Sinclair's boat yard and had set fire to the place on the same night. The files said that Rosco was a strange, moody sort of man. You could imagine him reacting to a difficult situation with a burst of violent temper. The court had accepted that Rosco had not known about the security officer's visiting the place.

"He probably did his boss a favour in the end," the officer in Bristol said. "The place is all yuppie flats now."

Wargan called Claire Bingham into his office, and she felt as she always did in his presence, like a naive schoolgirl.

"I can't see your problem," he said bluntly. "Why are you making such a meal of it? One of your suspects, Louis Rosco, has already killed a man after a sudden fit of violence. All you need is to find a connection between him and the victim. You should be concentrating all your energy on that. Don't bother with the rest of the bunch. Send them home if they want to go!"

"But Rosco didn't even know that Franks would be on the trip," Claire said. She knew she sounded shrill and defensive, but she wanted, more than anything, to complete the

121

investigation without Wargan's help or interference. He had told her too many times that a mother's place was with her children.

"How do you know that?" he demanded. "You've only Rosco's word for it. Young Franks was into drug dealing, and Rosco had a boat. Perhaps they were working together. You need proof that they knew each other, that's all."

He paused, and she watched him in the laborious process of thought. "Then there's the boat," he said. "How could an ex-con afford a boat like the *Jessie Ellen*? No bank's going to lend a penny to a man like that. Perhaps he was making his money from drugs, too."

He smiled unpleasantly, and she was afraid for a moment that he was going to reach out and pat her hand. She hated him most when he tried to be fatherly.

"Have Rosco in for questioning," he said. "If you can't handle him, I'll talk to him myself."

She was on her way to pick up Rosco when there was a phone call for her from George Palmer-Jones. George said that he was sorry, but he would not make it back to Cornwall after all tonight. There was an interesting lead which he felt he should follow. He was prepared to give her more details of his discovery, but her interview with Wargan had made her short-tempered. She said she was in a hurry and would speak to him on the following day.

Rosco had spent the afternoon at the cottage on the shore. He had been sawing a dead elm into logs, then splitting them with a heavy old-fashioned axe and stacking them in a honeycomb against the house, aware all the time that there was a uniformed policeman in the lane watching him. When Claire Bingham and Berry arrived, Rosco had put his axe away and was pegging out washing on the line in the small back garden, though by then it was almost dusk, and there was no chance of it's drying.

Rosco was not surprised to see the car driven carefully down the lane. He was surprised it had taken them so long to come for him. He thought it was tactics. They would want to make him sweat.

Claire walked round the cottage through the knee-deep grass to find him.

"Mr. Rosco," she said formally, "we'd like you to come with us to the police station to answer some questions."

He stood, poised in the fading light in the shadow of the trees, a peg in the hand stretched above his head.

"Can you give me a few minutes," he said, "to wash and shave?" He did not know how long he would be away.

She nodded, and she and Berry waited in the car for him because there was nowhere in the small cottage they could wait without disturbing his privacy. When he came out to them, he was wearing a clean shirt and black cord trousers. They switched on the car headlights as soon as he was at the door, and they could see him quite clearly. He was empty-handed. There was no gun dropped surreptitiously into the undergrowth between the house and the lane. That had been done hours ago.

Back in Heanor Claire insisted on talking to Rosco herself. They sat in the bare, squalid interview room, lit by a bright neon strip light, and throughout the conversation she felt uneasy. Even when she should have been pleased by his answers, she felt she was making a mistake. But she was young and inexperienced and could not trust the instinct which told her he was not a liar.

"Why didn't you tell us about your prison record?" she asked.

"It was something I wasn't particularly proud of." He had known it would come to this—the ugly interview room, the endless meaningless questions. All afternoon, with the saw and the axe, he had been trying to banish the memory of the last time.

"You must have known we'd find out," the inspector said.

"Yes," he said. He was looking down at the table. His face was brown, and she saw as his head bent that his hair was thinning and that the top of his head was brown, too. "When the boy died, I panicked," he said. "I thought it was an accident, and then all the questions started. It was like the last time. That was a terrible shock, too."

"But you were responsible for the security guard's death," she said. "You did start the fire at the boat yard?"

"Oh, yes," he said bitterly. "I started the fire." He paused. "But I wasn't responsible for young Franks' death. I had nothing to do with that."

"Why should I believe you now?"

He looked up at her, not expecting her to believe him, but wanting to explain. "I was happy," he said. "There was no reason for me to spoil it. Then he added, with his prisoner's resignation and hopelessness: "I should have known it was all too good to last."

She imagined the superintendent's sneering and refused to accept that he was telling her the truth.

"Where did you get the money for the *Jessie Ellen*?"

"It was a loan," he said, "from a friend."

"What was the name of this friend?"

He shook his head. "I can't tell you that."

"Was this friend involved in the arson on the boat yard?" she asked with a sudden flash of inspiration.

"No," he said. "Of course not. How could he be?"

"You could have been paid by someone else to set fire to the yard," she said.

"No. It wasn't like that." He paused, then continued. "Look, I've been asked questions like these before. By coppers a lot harder than you. I've served my sentence. Now it's my business."

"No," she said. "Now it's my business. You're a suspect in the investigation of a very serious case. And, as you said, now you've got more to lose. More than last time. This time there's a girlfriend. And a daughter."

He looked up sharply, and at first she thought he would deny it. Then pride and a possessive tenderness took over. She could imagine him showing snaps of Matilda to strangers.

"So you know about that?" he said.

She nodded.

"Leave them out of this," he said. "Rose knew nothing."

"She knows you've been to prison."

"Yes," he said. "She knows that. I've not lied to her."

"She means a lot to you," the inspector said.

124

"Yes," he cried. "She means a lot to me."

"You'd do almost anything to keep her."

"She's not mine to keep."

"Then you'd do almost anything to make her yours."

The superintendent would laugh when he heard that on the tape, she thought. "My God, woman!" he'd say. "You talk like a romantic novel."

There was a silence, and then suddenly he was shouting. "I didn't kill the boy!"

A policeman outside the door looked in to see if Claire needed help. She shook her head briefly, and the constable went away.

"When did you leave prison?" she asked with a calm formality.

"You've got the records," he said angrily. "You know better than me."

"Almost four years ago to the day," she said. "What did you do?"

"I bought the boat in Bristol," he said, "and I came home."

"You bought the boat," she said. "Just like that!"

"It took some time to find what I wanted," he said, choosing to misunderstand the question. "And to sort out the loan from my friend."

"How much time?"

He shrugged. "Six months."

"Where did you stay during that six months?"

"With friends in Bristol. Different friends. I moved around a lot."

"Did you report to a probation officer during that time?" He nodded. "I was on parole," he said. "I wasn't going to take any risks. I couldn't see the point of it, but I did as I was told."

"Where did you go?"

"To the office in White Heath, just outside Bristol. A friend from the prison lived on the estate there."

"What was the name of your probation officer?" Claire Bingham held her breath, convinced for a moment that he would name Jane Pym. There were so many coincidences in

125

this case that one more seemed inevitable. But Rosco shook his head, unaware of her tension.

"I can't remember," he said. "It was a man. Young. Straight out of college. I expect there'll be records somewhere."

"And when you left prison," she asked, "did you go to stay with your mysterious friends immediately?"

"No," he said. "Not straight away. They couldn't put me up straight away. The welfare officer in the nick found me a place for a while. In a probation hostel. I wasn't there for long. There was a fire, and they moved everyone out."

Then there was the inevitable coincidence. Claire had discovered the link between Louis Rosco and Greg Franks which Wargan was so certain existed. She sat back in her chair and regarded the man with wonder and pity. It was as if he had convicted himself.

"Can you remember any of the other residents at the hostel?" she asked.

"No," he said with indifference. "They were mostly youngsters. I didn't mix much."

Again she was astounded by the folly of his confession. It was possible, of course, that he had no memory of meeting Greg Franks in the hostel, though the memory of the fire meant they must have been there at the same time. Alternatively, if he was the killer and the murder stemmed from the meeting four years before, perhaps he thought it wise to admit to staying there. If he was not aware that all the records had been lost in the fire, he would assume that the police would find out anyway. Most likely, she thought, looking at his brown, blank, ordinary face, he had been trapped by a coincidence the superintendent would never believe, and for a moment she felt ashamed of her part in it. She even considered letting him go back to the cottage, but she had her career to think of and decided it would be safer to keep him there. They would have to search the place before they allowed him back.

In Myrtle Cottage they were sitting round the table after a late supper when the car came to take Jane Pym to the police station. Rose had cleared most of the plates but had become distracted halfway through the task, and there were still empty wine bottles, glasses, a plate of cheese, a bowl of fruit. During the meal there was little conversation. Each person seemed preoccupied with his own thoughts. They talked in occasional bursts about the weather, foreign travel, and with more commitment about seabirds. Roger reported Gwen Pullen's theory that the petrel had come from an isolated colony on the Aleutian Islands and discussed ideas for raising money for an expedition during the following breeding season. It was as if murder, the wearing day's interviews, had never taken place. They were tired and drained.

The first interruption to the evening came with George's phone call to Molly. Rose answered it quickly, as if she were expecting the telephone to ring, then called Molly to the phone. When Molly returned to the table, the others looked at her eagerly, though they were too polite, too exhausted, to ask for news. They knew about George's reputation and hoped for some miraculous end to their misery. They were like a group of ex-patriots trapped in some bleak and hostile country, waiting for information from the civilised world. George had escaped the tedious police questioning and the irritation of continuous shared company. They were a little jealous and thought he should be there to endure it with them.

"He's not coming back tonight," Molly said, and sensed their disappointment, "He said the traffic's too heavy. It's the bank holiday."

"I'm sorry," Roger Pym said languidly. "It would have been pleasant to have someone new to talk to."

"Where will he stay?" Rose asked. She seemed obliged still to look after them all.

"There's an hotel," Molly said. "It's near the village where he was phoning from. I think it's called Rashwood Hall. Do you know it, Duncan? It must be quite close to your home."

Startled from thought of his own, surprised, it seemed, to be spoken to, James blinked and nodded.

Yes, he said. He had heard of it. He hoped George would be comfortable there.

"What will the inspector say about his not coming back?"

Jane Pym asked. "She didn't seem very positive when I asked when we could go home." She was very tense, petulant. She would have liked to explain the importance of her work, to tell them it was vital she return, but the words would not come, and embarrassed, she shrank back into her seat. No one gave her an answer.

Later, when the meal was over and they could think of nothing more to say, the sound of the front doorbell came as a relief.

"Perhaps old George has made it back after all," Roger Pym said. Then the others joined in with a desperate optimism. Perhaps the traffic had cleared. Perhaps George had heard the long-term weather forecast which predicted the tail end of hurricane Erin crossing the Atlantic with a series of heavy depressions. George liked seabirds more than any of them. He would not want to miss a good blow.

Only Jane Pym remained silent, as if she had a premonition of what was to follow. She watched Rose Pengelly leave the table to answer the door.

The sight of Sergeant Berry, quiet, apologetic but somehow intimidating in his calm, stopped the chatter. He said that Inspector Bingham was sorry to interrupt their evening, but she would be grateful if she could have a few words with Mrs. Pym. He had a car with him and would bring her back when the interview was over. It was only a routine matter, and they weren't to worry at all.

Jane Pym stared at the sergeant, bewildered and unmoving. It was Roger who replied first. "I'll come, too," he said. "I'll not have you bullying Jane. She'll need someone with her."

"No need for that," Berry said; his voice was firm and gentle. "I'll look after her for you."

And before anyone else could protest, Jane walked towards the sergeant, as if in a trance, and was out of the room. They heard the front door slam and the car drive away. There was a silence.

Molly could sense then a general frustration. The remaining people were more awake, quite excited. Most of the gathering wished that Roger would leave the table. They were

128

eager to discuss the implication of Jane's summons, to indulge in the delight and relief of gossip, but it was hardly tactful to speculate that a woman might be a murderer while her husband was sitting in the same room.

Claire had asked to speak to the woman because she thought she might remember Rosco from the hostel and fill in the gaps from the records lost in the fire. But as the interview progressed, she became aware slowly that the woman had been drinking. At first she seemed quite calm and controlled. She showed little resentment at having been dragged from her supper table out into the night. She did seem to Claire to have aged since the interview in the morning. The lines on her forehead were more noticeable, her hair more lank and untidy. She was easier to intimidate.

Then the indications of drunkenness became more apparent. Listening to the inspector's patient questions, Jane's eyes glazed, and Claire had to repeat herself. She mumbled occasional replies. Some of her responses were slightly incoherent and irrational. There were bursts of aggression. Claire wondered then if she had been taking drugs rather than alcohol, but Jane was a respected probation officer, and at first the idea seemed impossible.

"You told me that you worked for a while at the probation hostel in Bristol," the inspector said.

"Yes," Jane said. "Just for a few months while the warden was on maternity leave."

"Can you tell me when that was?"

There was a pause and a mumbled reply, so the inspector had to repeat the question.

"Four years ago, I think," Jane said. Her head was spinning, and she was finding it impossible to plan what to say. "Yes, it was in the summer four years ago."

"And you think you saw Greg Franks there?"

"I thought so," Jane said. "I was almost sure. You'd be able to check on his records. There must be a file somewhere, even if he wasn't convicted."

"We've been in touch with the hostel," Claire said, "but apparently there was a fire, and all the records were lost. It makes things difficult."

129

"Yes," Jane said. She was staring vacantly in front of her. "I remember the fire. It was just after I left. I'm sure the wardens have done everything they can to help the police. . . ." Her voice faded into incoherence.

"It's a pity they've not been more effective," Claire said. "Though I suppose it's not their responsibility. Neither of them was there four years ago. None of the field officers can remember Franks, either, though."

Then Jane Pym's voice changed and became sharp and hostile, as if Claire had insulted her personally. "You can't blame probation officers for not remembering all their clients," she said. "If you knew how many people we see in a year. Some men only stopped in the hostel for a few days. And we do hundreds of social enquiry reports on people coming up to court. It's a thankless enough job as it is without all this criticism."

Claire ignored the anger. "Could one of the men who stayed in the hostel that summer have been Louis Rosco?" she asked. She was beginning to wonder if Jane Pym was being deliberately obstructive, to imagine even some form of collaboration between the woman and the two clients of the probation service. Her caseload must be full of addicts, and the opportunity of dealing in drugs would be enormous.

"Why?" Jane Pym asked suddenly. She was shocked, it seemed, out of her alcoholic blur. "Was he there?"

"So he says. He remembers the fire, so it must have been at the same time as Greg."

"No," Jane said slowly. "I don't remember. As I've told you, I had left before the fire. Perhaps I'd gone before he arrived."

"Doesn't that seem rather an odd coincidence? That three of you on the *Jessie Ellen* might have been together in a probation hostel in Bristol and no one recognised each other?"

"I recognised Greg," Jane said defensively. "I thought I knew him."

"But not Rosco?"

"No!" But the idea of Louis Rosco seemed to trouble her, and she withdrew into a dispirited and unhelpful lethargy, answering the inspector's questions with monosyllables, making it clear that she only wanted the interview to be over.

Jane was driven home by a uniformed policewoman she had never seen before, and the journey passed in silence. She was pleased. Sergeant Berry made her feel strangely and irrationally guilty, and she felt that in his presence there was a danger she would break down and confess to grave and unimagined sins. The constable dropped her outside Myrtle Cottage, then drove on down the valley to turn the car. Jane stood outside the house, breathing deeply, trying to compose herself before going inside. It was still not late, and she pictured them all there, as she had left them, sitting round the kitchen table waiting with a ghoulish excitement to find out what had happened, perhaps even to accuse her. She suspected that Roger's offer to accompany her to the police station was caused by curiosity rather than a wish to give her support. It was a pleasant surprise when she lifted the latch on the kitchen door to find the room empty. The living room beyond was dark and quiet, too. They had been so exhausted that everyone, even Roger, must have given up waiting and gone to bed.

She sat in the dark on the rocking chair in the kitchen and began to cry.

The old woman must have been standing in the doorway for some time before Jane realised she was there. She stood, quite unembarrassed by the tears, and made no move to come into the room or retreat. When she saw Jane look up, she spoke.

"Was it quite dreadful!" she said.

"I suppose not," she said. "Just confusing."

"Tell me," Molly said.

Then the temptation to spill it all out was too much, and Jane explained about Greg and Rosco having been at the hostel, about the fire which had destroyed the records.

"I was there, too," Jane said. "I was working in the hostel that summer. The warden was on maternity leave, and I took over. The inspector thinks it's too much of a coincidence, and that I must in some way be implicated."

Molly said nothing. She allowed Jane her righteous indig-

131

nation. But she thought the inspector was probably right. The coincidence was incredible.

Molly went to her room then, but she could not sleep. She tried to piece together the overheard conversations, the whispered confessions, the suppressed antagonism, to make some pattern, but it was impossible. At some time after midnight there was a knock on her door, and Rose stood there, like the heroine of some Victorian bodice-ripper, in a long white nightgown and a white shawl. Her hair was tangled and untidy, and there was mud on the hem of her nightdress.

"Come in," Molly said mildly. "What's the matter?"

"It's Louis," Rose said. She began to cry. "They've taken him into custody."

"Have they charged him?"

"I don't think so. I don't know."

"What happened?"

Then Rose began to talk, the words spilling out in random phrases. It was part of a declaration of love, part an explanation of her fear, and only when Molly prompted her, did it become a detailed account of what had happened that evening.

"I didn't realise," she said, "how much I cared for him. I mean, I fancied him right from the beginning, from the moment he moved into the cottage and I saw him down there, working on the *Jessie Ellen*, getting her ready for the sea. I mean, I knew then that I wanted to have his baby. But that was all. I didn't want to get involved. I'd been hurt before. Only safe, unfanciable men like Gerald Matthews for me, I thought. I told Louis that. No involvement, I said, I can't handle involvement. He told me he'd been to prison. I wasn't surprised. I mean, there were so many rumours in Heanor about him, I'd have been ready to believe anything. Now look at me. I'm as involved as hell."

"What has happened?" Molly asked again. "Where have you been?"

"Down to the cottage, of course," Rose said. "I heard the cars go down some time ago. I thought it was the police bringing Louis home. But you should see what they're doing there! They're going through the cottage searching his things.

They think he killed Greg Franks. I came back here and phoned the police station. They told me they were keeping Louis in custody overnight.''

She began to cry. Molly could tell that the hours of waiting for Louis to return to Porthkennan had been a terrible strain.

"You must do something," she said. "Louis didn't kill Greg. He had no reason to. You can help us. I know about you and George. Everyone who comes to stay talks about the Tom French murder. Please get Louis home for me."

Molly waited until the tears and hysteria had subsided.

"Rose," she said. "Was Greg Franks blackmailing Louis about his criminal record?"

"No," Rose said. "That's why I'm so certain Louis didn't kill him. Greg Franks was blackmailing *me*."

"Why?"

"He had found out somehow who was Matilda's father," Rose said. "He said he would tell the birding world I was screwing a convicted killer. 'Who would want to stay in Myrtle Cottage then?' he said. And 'Who would trust Rosco to take them out in a boat?' "

"How did he know Louis had been convicted of manslaughter?"

"He met him in Bristol in some hostel."

"Are you sure he didn't approach Louis for money, too?"

"No," she said. "I think he was a bit frightened of Louis." She paused. "Gerald knew something was going on," she said. "He hated Greg and made me promise not to have him here again. But I couldn't turn him away. I didn't know what he would do."

"Did Gerald ever confront Greg? Tell him to keep away?"

"No," Rose said scornfully. "He wouldn't have the guts."

Then Rose, wallowing in her muddled emotion, began to plead with Molly again to do something to free Louis so he could be returned to her. But Molly made no promise, and it was only when she had the phone call from the hospital that she decided to take more direct action.

When the superintendent discovered the link between Rosco and Franks, he was jubilant. That was enough to keep

Rosco in custody at least overnight, he said. In the meantime they would have a look at his cottage. If they could find any illegal substances, it would all be over. But the search of the cottage on the shore ended up as a farce. No one had considered that there might not be electricity, and the lanterns they found were beyond them to operate.

They plundered the place, like burglars with torches, feeling through the drawers of the heavy old chest in the bedroom, stacking tins of soup from the kitchen cupboard in the middle of the floor. Berry lifted the mattress on the bed and felt the frame beneath, and his fingers came away scratched by rust. There was no gun.

Although it was very late when Inspector Bingham returned to the house in the smart new estate on the hill, Richard was waiting up for her. She could tell immediately that he was angry and that in the hours of waiting he had stoked the fury with distant wrongs and imagined hurts.

"Where the hell have you been?" he demanded. "I've been worried stiff."

"I'm sorry," she said. It was much better, she had discovered, to apologise immediately. Sometimes an apology was enough to satisfy him, and he would become calm and gracious. "I should have phoned."

Tonight, however, the apology was insufficient. He had obviously been waiting, brooding on all the things he would say to her when she got in, the painful home truths it would be good for her to hear.

She had hardly walked through the door when he began his lecture.

"It's a matter of priorities," he said, so quickly that she knew the sentence had been rehearsed. "I mean, I don't expect to come first—I'm only your husband after all—but what about your son? You haven't seen him for days."

"I'm sorry," she said again. "We've taken someone into custody. It should be over soon."

But that still wasn't good enough. All the old niggling criticisms, which at another time she might have found amusing, were dragged into the row. There was the lack of ironed shirts, her failure *ever* to cook anything that hadn't come out of a microwave or a freezer, the drawer in his chest full of odd socks.

"Didn't you realise that Mrs. Newby's on holiday this week?" he demanded. Mrs. Newby came in twice a week to dust and Hoover and empty the dishwasher. "The house is collapsing around us. And damm it! I had a meeting of the round table, and I couldn't go."

Then she was joyously and rewardingly furious. He was like a little boy, she said, deprived of some treat. Why did men never grow up? Was he incapable of ironing shirts and cooking meals? And when it came to priorities, she happened to think that catching a murderer was a little more important than the bloody round table. She stormed to the bedroom and fell suddenly and deeply asleep. When he came to bed some time later to make his peace with her, to make love to her, she was so exhausted that he could not wake her. It was only much later that the sound of the telephone's ringing disturbed her. She picked it up half-asleep, hardly aware of where she was, and some unfamiliar voice informed her that George Palmer-Jones had been the victim of a hit-and-run accident and was in a Bristol hospital.

11

George was rescued by a woman with a passion for foxes. She lived in a basement flat in the house nearest to the alley and put out food for them. Each night she would sit in the dark watching the foxes come into the small backyard to pick fussily at the chicken bones and left-over meat she laid out for them on the dirty flags. She claimed she could easily recognise individuals. Sometimes they were too hungry for her delicacies and went straight to the bins left out in the alley. Then she would leave the flat and go out into the yard to look at them there. She led a nocturnal existence, staying awake late into the night and not getting up until lunchtime.

So, when she heard the clatter of dustbins late that night, she thought it was her foxes and went out immediately to see them. The sight of the man, obviously injured, lying where the animals should have been playing confused her. She had little contact with people. She did not know what to do. When he opened his eyes and looked at her, she felt trapped.

"Are you ill?" she called from a safe distance. She was still wearing her carpet slippers. George, lying in pain with his head close to the ground, could see them.

"I think you should call an ambulance," he said.

Glad then for permission to return to the safety of her flat, she sauntered away. Her son had paid for her telephone, and she rarely used it, so it was with some difficulty that she was connected to the ambulance service. When the call was over, she felt quite proud of herself and waited, still in the dark, to watch for the flashing lights and noise of the ambulance. With all that commotion she was sure her foxes would not return that night.

George woke up in hospital from a deep sleep that had more to do with tranquilisers and painkillers than peace of mind, to the antiseptic smell of the ward and two women on chairs by the side of the bed. Molly had insisted that Claire Bingham be told of George's injuries. It must, she said, be relevant. George had decided to stay in Bristol for another day because of a promising lead to the enquiry. Nothing trivial would keep him in the town. The weather map showed there was a big storm brewing, and only something important would keep him from the seawatching.

Wargan had given his blessing to Claire's trip to the city, more, she thought, because he hoped she would make a fool of herself than because he believed anything could be achieved.

"Go if you like," he said. "But I can't see that it's relevant."

"Palmer-Jones was working for the Franks family," she said. "And now he's the victim of a hit-and-run accident."

"We've got our man," he insisted. "We'll take him out to the cottage and search it properly by daylight."

"You'll have to charge him soon," Claire said, but Wargan was convinced that they would have evidence to convict him by the end of the day.

The ward sister regarded the group round Palmer-Jones with suspicion and hostility. Usually visitors would not be allowed on the ward in the morning. Only the inspector's warrant card had persuaded her to let them in at all. Now they were huddled together in serious conversation, blocking the way of the domestic staff, causing jealousy and resentment in those patients whose relatives had been turned away. Once she went up to the group and vented her anger.

"You can't stay much longer," she said. "Mr. Palmer-Jones has had a nasty shock. He's not a young man anymore. Besides, the doctor will be here to see him soon."

But the women took no notice of her, and the conference,

the sharing of information and ideas, continued. George sat up in bed, looking quite unfamiliar in hospital pyjamas. His face was badly bruised.

"What happened?" Claire Bingham asked. "Was it an accident?"

"No," George said. "It was no accident." He explained about the cheque sent from Cranmers to Greg Franks. "Someone thought I needed scaring off."

"But who?" Claire said. "Not Duncan James. He wouldn't organise a thing like that."

"Oh, no," George said. "It wasn't Duncan James. Anne James probably phoned Duncan and told him I'd been asking questions, but you're right. Duncan wouldn't go in for violence. Presumably he panicked and got in touch with Barnes. I think the stunt with the car was Barnes' idea. Someone capable of turning Rashwood Hall into such a hideous mess would be capable of anything. Think how it must have seemed to him when I turned up at Rashwood Hall and then went home with his personal assistant. I booked a room at the hall in my own name."

"Do you think the assault on you is connected in any way with the Franks murder?"

"Not necessarily. James probably hadn't told Barnes he was being blackmailed by Greg. I'd guess he'd want as little contact with the developer as possible. Barnes might have organised last night's 'accident' just because he didn't want it widely known that he had bribed an officer of the Nature Conservancy Council to withhold information which would have made Rashwood Park declared a site of scientific interest."

"I'm here officially to check on Rosco," Claire said. "It does seem a remarkable coincidence that he and Franks should have met four years ago."

"I don't know if it was coincidence or design," George said, and told them about his conversation with Vicky Jones. "Greg seems to have taken a perverse and mischievous pleasure in bringing together people who disliked him," he said. "He could have provoked any one of them to murder."

By the time the doctor arrived and the sister triumphantly

shepherded the women from the ward, they had formed a plan of campaign for the day.

Claire Bingham went south to the city centre. On the road from Heanor to Bristol she had experienced a crisis of confidence which, if Molly Palmer-Jones had not been sitting beside her, she would have blown up out of all proportion. She might even have called it a breakdown. It happened on the M5 just outside Exeter, but it must have been brewing for days, since she was given the responsibility for the Franks murder investigation. Then, driving at speed on the outside lane of the motorway, she had been conscious, with a sudden, dizzying self-awareness, that nothing in her life was working properly. She had a vision of the disparate elements of her life as mechanical components exploding away from her, as in the slow-motion film of a bombed car. Before, she felt, she had managed to keep things together with an effort of will. Now she had lost control of it all. Later she was to put the experience down to exhaustion or shock. Her husband realised, too, that it was close to the anniversary of her mother's death. At the time she was terrified, and though she continued to drive up the motorway, passing lorries and caravans like an automaton, she thought she was insane and knew she would never take responsibility for anything again.

"I think we should stop for coffee at the next services, don't you?" Molly Palmer-Jones said. Claire never knew if the suggestion was coincidental, or if Molly had sensed her sudden tension. "And breakfast—it must be breakfast time by now."

So, obediently Claire had turned the car off the motorway into the service station. She looked at the car clock and saw that the time was eight o'clock. Even from the car they could smell the bacon frying in the transport café where the lorry drivers were eating in smoky isolation. But once she had switched off the ignition, Claire could not move. She was rigid, her knuckles white as they gripped the steering wheel, her neck and shoulders braced against the back of the car seat.

"My dear," Molly said, "What is the matter?"

If anyone else had asked the same question, Claire would

139

have shook her head and remained stiff and tight-lipped. But the elderly woman's interest and understanding allowed her to speak. It all came out, the impossibility of living with Richard, the impossibility of working with Wargan, her guilt and frustration. Her life, she said at last, was one massive cock-up.

The most miraculous thing about the whole encounter, she later told Richard, was that by the end of it they were both laughing. They laughed at the pomposity of men and the weakness of women who were taken in by it, and at Claire herself for taking them too seriously. Claire was never sure how the tension had been released and confidence restored. Molly had listened but said very little. There was no physical contact, no comforting embrace. But at the end the crisis was over, and she felt able to start again.

"Coffee," Molly said. "Now we definitely need coffee. And mounds of toast."

So they walked across the car park to the cafeteria, with its piped music and the smell of baking bread pumped specially from the kitchen to make the place appear welcoming. Then they sat at a quiet table gossiping, more like mother and daughter than like strangers.

Claire Bingham's loss of nerve on the M5 was to prove a turning point in the case, though they never discussed it again. There were no longer two separate and parallel investigations. She found herself prepared to listen to Molly's ideas and trust her judgement. By the time they had the conference with George in the hospital, she was open to his theory that Duncan James had been blackmailed by Greg Franks over the Rashwood development. She listened carefully to the views of Molly and George and found they had quite different ideas about how the case would be resolved. With the experience on the motorway, her hero worship had returned. She was prepared to consider a flexibility in her methods which would have astounded her colleagues at Heanor, who saw her as a mindless follower of rules.

It was Claire who charmed and wheedled information and reminiscences from the retired policeman who had looked into the fire at Sinclair's boat yard. It was Claire who came up with the ultimate coincidence.

She went first to the police station in the city centre where Rosco had been charged with arson and manslaughter. A middle-aged detective constable was waiting for her, but she soon gathered that Wargan, who had arranged the visit by phone, had not described it as of any urgency or importance.

"Just background you wanted, according to your superintendent," the D.C. said, pulling a chair for her up to his cluttered desk. "There won't be many people working here who remember the case now. Everything's changed."

"What have you got in the way of background?" she asked, and he brought out a few tatty pieces of paper, case notes, photocopies of which she had already seen.

"Is that all?" she said. "There must be something else. Someone who remembers the Rosco case. It was a big fire. It must have stuck in people's memories."

And because she was attractive and smiled at him, he made coffee for them both and talked to her. He told her about Hubert Rolfe, the detective sergeant who had never believed Rosco had planned the fire by himself, and who had made such a nuisance of himself about the case that he was forced to take early retirement.

"Not a popular man, Hubert Rolfe," the detective said. "Not here." He looked around him to check that no one was listening. "Too straight sometimes for his own good. He's a great one for causes. Now he's got a bee in his bonnet about the development of the docks. Says it's changed the character of the city. You often see letters from him in the paper."

"I'd like to speak to Rolfe," Claire said. "Where does he live? Would he speak to me?"

"He still lives in Bedminster," the detective said. "I believe he and his wife bought the police house there before he retired. If he's not at home, he'll be on the bowling green. His wife will point you in the right direction. And he'll speak to you. He'll speak to anyone that'll listen."

She walked out into the sunshine, into a busy shopping street and through the centre, past Saint Mary Radcliffe Church towards the river. It was a place of prosperity and style, of warehouses with newly scrubbed brickwork turned into offices for computer firms, of attractive wine bars and expensive apartments overlooking the water. Outside the Arnol Fini Arts Centre a student was handing out publicity about a university production of *The Duchess of Malfi*. It was the sort of place where Claire Bingham felt at home.

She crossed the river by a narrow footbridge close to the SS *Great Britain* and found Rolfe's home almost immediately. It was semidetached, neat, immaculately cared for, the pebble dash facing newly white washed. At the other end of the road she could see the red brick bulk of the old Wills' tobacco factory. This was a different Bristol from the elegance of Clifton or the affluence of the docks. She might have been in industrial Lancashire. There were net curtains at the windows, and as she walked up the street, she felt she was being watched.

When Claire Bingham knocked at the door, it was opened by a tiny woman in a flowery nylon overall with a duster in her hand. From the open door came the smell of newly cleaned windows and furniture polish.

"I'm sorry, my dear," Mrs. Rolfe said, hardly looking at the caller, her attention still inside where the brasses needed doing. "Hubert's not here. He never is in the mornings. Not in this weather. You'll find him in the park. On the bowling green." And she closed the door firmly on the dirty, uncertain world outside.

The park could have been in a northern town, too. It was small, rather scruffy, bordered on one side by allotments. There were rusting wrought iron lamp posts and elderly ladies walking threadbare dogs in the sun. In contrast the bowling green was perfectly smooth, and there was a smart new pavilion at one end. Outside the pavilion she asked a ferocious woman dressed in the club uniform of grey skirt and blazer for Hubert and was directed disapprovingly to a bench by the green. With the uniform the woman seemed to have taken on a prefect's bossiness, and throughout her conversation with Hubert Rolfe, Claire could hear her calling orders and encouragement to her partner.

Hubert Rolfe was dozing on one of the iron benches which

had been set along the edge of the green. He might have begun to watch the game, but when Claire reached him, his eyes were shut and he was snoring gently. When she woke him, he startled but remained in the same position, his legs stretched out before him, his head tilted slightly back.

"Who are you?" he asked sharply. "What do you want?" His voice had strong Lancastrian vowels, and she thought he would always feel himself a stranger in this city.

She showed him her warrant card. "I wanted to ask for your help," she said. "It's about Louis Rosco."

"Why? I thought he was out. What's he been up to now?"

"He's been taken into custody in Cornwall. A young man was drowned, and it's turned out to be murder. My superintendent thinks Rosco is responsible."

"It doesn't sound likely to me," Rolfe said. Claire thought he must have cultivated his north-country accent for years, determined not to be taken for one of those west-country yokels. "Rosco's no murderer. Not unless he's changed."

"Tell me about the original offence," she said. "Tell me about the fire."

Then at last he sat upright and alert on the bench, no longer half-asleep with his eyes closed against the sun. He looked more like a soldier than a policeman. His hair was shaved very short at the back and sides, and he had a small grey moustache. She came to realise that he was slightly mad.

"The city around the docks was a different place then," he said. "That was before the developers got their hands on it. There were rough pubs, still a lot of derelict land after the war, a few old girls on the game. . . . Not that what we've got now is any improvement."

She nodded to show she was listening but knew he would have to tell the story in his own way.

"Then there was the boat yard," he said. "Sinclair's boat yard. The owner was a Scot. It wasn't a flash place, but it was known for the quality of the workmanship. Mostly it took on refits, repairs, and occasionally they would be commissioned to do a one-off." He looked at her strangely. "I used to call in there a lot," he said. "I like boats. I had

143

dreams at one time of building one myself, taking off around the world. But there was always work and the kids to feed. And now I'm too old."

He paused, trying to re-create the excitement of the old dream and failing. "I used to call in," he repeated, "so I knew Rosco before he was arrested for the fire. I had a lot of time for him. He was a grafter. Not showy but reliable."

He paused again and clapped as the loud woman in the grey blazer put a bowl close to the jack.

"Then Sinclair wanted to expand," he continued. "I can't remember the details. Not now. There was a big order, apparently, that he couldn't meet without new equipment. So he took on a new partner. Someone who wanted to buy into a successful local business. At least that's what he said at the time."

Now she did feel she should interrupt.

"But if he was such a good worker, and the business was expanding, why did they make Rosco redundant?"

He looked at her. "Well," he said, "that's the big question, isn't it? That's what I wanted to know."

"And did you come up with an answer?" she asked, knowing already that he would have, because he was the sort of man to worry at a problem until he had come up with a solution.

"Oh, yes," he said. "I came up with an answer. Rosco was sacked because that gave him a good excuse for setting fire to the yard."

"But why?" she cried, although she thought she had already guessed.

"It was an insurance fraud," Rolfe said, and waited, as if he expected applause. "An elaborate insurance fraud."

"But why did Rosco go along with the plan?" Claire asked.

"He was made an offer he couldn't refuse," Rolfe said. "After the Rosco case I made it my business to find out about the businessman Sinclair took into the boat yard as a sleeping partner. More like a gangster than a businessman, I found out. Involved in all sorts of unsavoury business. But wanting to go respectable. And desperate for land so he could have a piece of the action in the dock development. I should think he'd have some powerful means of persuasion.''

Rolfe looked at her to make sure she was listening intently.

''When the security guard was killed, Sinclair's partner might have been afraid Rosco would tell us everything. But Rosco didn't. And I don't think it was because he was scared. He'd been promised money, a lot of money, when he got out. Louis and I got quite close after all the interviews—you know how you sometimes do—and he almost admitted to me once why he'd got involved in the deal. 'You like boats, Sergeant Rolfe,' he said. 'Haven't you ever felt you'd do nearly anything for a boat of your own?' He thought he'd get a boat out of it when it was all over. I knew what he meant, but it wasn't the sort of thing you could use as evidence.''

''Who was the businessman?'' Claire asked. ''What was his name?''

''Barnes,'' Rolfe said with disgust, and there had been so many other coincidences in the case that it came as no surprise. It could be no one else. ''Brian Barnes. He runs a company called Squirrel.''

''Yes,'' she said. ''I know. I've heard of it.''

''He's a bloody millionaire,'' Rolfe said. ''If it's the last thing I do, I want him behind bars. I can't stand him.'' He nodded towards the smartly painted pavilion, where most of the spectators of the match were sitting in the shade. ''Barnes gave a donation to the club to build that place,'' he said. ''That's why I'm sitting out here with the sun in my eyes and why the wife makes me a flask and sandwiches for my dinner. I'll not set foot in it.''

''Do you think Barnes still sees Rosco as a threat?''

''I do. It would suit him fine if Rosco was locked up again. While he's out, there's always a risk of him talking.''

''Tell me about Barnes,'' she said. ''Everything you know about him.''

''It'll take a while,'' he said. ''I've been studying him for years.'' She realised then that his dislike of Barnes was unreasonable, unbalanced, an obsession.

''Why do you bother?'' she asked. ''You're out of it now.''

''I needn't be,'' he said suddenly. ''They threw me out

145

because of Barnes. I'll never prove it, but I know all the same. The deputy chief constable has been a friend of Barnes' for years. He and the family go every year to stay in Barnes' villa in the Algarve, and now he's a member of that posh country club at Rashwood Hall. They called it early retirement on health grounds, but it was the sack just the same. I was a good policeman."

"Go on," she said. "Tell me about him."

When he started speaking, she was amazed by the detail of his information and the fact that he could remember it all. He had stored up the story of the man's life, fueling his bitterness by recalling the number of Barnes' houses, the extent of his business empire, his wealth, and his influence.

She took notes in shorthand and listened, astounded, as he painted a picture of the man he was convinced had lost him his job.

"He's a single man," Rolfe said. "Never seemed to need the company of women, as far as I can see. Only money. He needs money as you and I need to breathe. He started off with a couple of betting shops here in Bedminster. I don't know how he got the finance for those. It's a long time ago. The big break came for him with his deal with Sinclair. When the boat yard went up in flames, he had the insurance and the land. Everyone at that time knew of the plans to develop the docks. He held on to the land, bought out Sinclair, and when the development corporation was formed with their plans for all those expensive houses, he was in a prime position. It's impossible to guess how much he made in that deal. Enough to buy more land in the middle of town and put up a load of houses and a hotel. Now he seems to have shares in every successful business in the city. There's that country club out at Rashwood in Somerset, and I heard last week that he's offered for a chain of local travel agents."

"Where does he live?" she asked.

"I don't think there's anything he calls home," Rolfe said. "Not really. There's a suite in the hotel in the city, and he spends a lot of time at the place at Rashwood. He has land in Scotland where he and his cronies go shooting grouse in the autumn, and a cottage in Cornwall for the sailing."

"Where in Cornwall?" she asked, and he looked at her sharply, excited, realizing the implication of the question.

"Near Heanor," he said. "Fremington Creek. Like I said, he goes there for the sailing."

"Rosco sails out of Heanor," she said. "It could be coincidence."

"Pigs might fly," he said.

"Barnes wouldn't have killed an innocent boy just to put Rosco in prison again," she said. "There'd be no need. Rosco's been out for four years, and he's caused Barnes no trouble. He got the *Jessie Ellen* out of the deal. As you said, that would be enough for him. Besides, how could Barnes have done it? He wasn't there."

"You could find out if Barnes was involved," Rolfe said, and he spoke so quickly that she realised he had been hatching such a plot for years, brooding about it. The details would be revised to meet this situation, but the general thrust of this means of revenge would be well known to him. To carry it out was the dream which had replaced the dream of sailing round the world. It had kept him going, kept him active and prepared.

"How?" she asked despite herself. She knew she should not encourage him.

"Release Rosco from custody," he said. "Then I'll start some rumours that Rosco's talked to the police about the Sinclair fire, and you're considering reopening the case. I'll say he had to give you information about the arson to persuade you that he had nothing to do with the Franks murder. That'll scare Barnes. That will flush him out for you. He'll want to shut Rosco up before the case comes to court."

"I can't do that," she said, shocked. "I can't put Rosco in that sort of danger."

"Why not?" Rolfe said, and she knew then that bitterness had made him insane. "If Barnes finishes off Rosco, you can do him for murder."

"I won't do it," she said, but she was fascinated all the same with the details of his plan. "How would you start the rumours?"

He shrugged. "I've still got informants," he said. "Peo-

147

ple who work for Barnes. They worked for me when I was in the force, and they still do. The money's just the same to them, whether it comes from my pocket or petty cash.

"Barnes would never believe them," she said.

"He might. If he's scared enough."

And he's scared already, Claire thought, with George Palmer-Jones' turning up at Rashwood Hall. For a moment she was tempted to go along with the idea. There was some attraction in having a quick, if dangerous, end to the case, but she knew it would not do.

"No," she said. "I can't allow it. It's far too risky."

"Suit yourself," he said, and lay back on the bench, his eyes narrowed against the sun, watching the smooth underarm action of the bowler. She was surprised by his compliance. She had expected him to put up more of a fight.

"Well," she said, standing, "thanks for the information anyway." But he seemed not to hear her and did not answer.

It was only when she was on her way past the pavilion that he spoke, and by then she was well out of earshot.

"It's not up to you to allow me anything, lady. I'm not a policeman now. I can do what I bloody well choose."

12

When Molly left the hospital, she went to White Heath. The name had recurred throughout the investigation. Roger Pym taught games at White Heath Comprehensive School. Jane Pym worked from an office there. Louis Rosco had stayed with friends on the White Heath Estate when he was first released from prison and reported to a probation officer based there under the terms of his parole. More recently, with Claire Bingham's help, Molly had traced the woman who had been in charge of the bail hostel to White Heath. It seemed that she had been promoted and the year before had been appointed senior to the team of probation officers. Molly thought that the place was worth a visit. It was a sign of Claire Bingham's new attitude to the case that she allowed the older woman to go alone.

The bus Molly caught was almost empty. The smart shops in the city centre would have little to offer the residents of White Heath. There were a few listless youths who had been in town to sign on the dole. They stared out of the window and had little to say even to each other. The bus dropped her at the edge of the estate by a primary school that looked like a prison. There were half a dozen tower blocks surrounded by a crescent of low level terraces. As she stepped out into the street, she felt suddenly chill, although the day was still fine. The weather was already starting to change. There were feathers of cloud which occasionally blocked the sun and a westerly breeze which blew litter across the streets and around the flats.

Molly found the probation office in the centre of the estate, in a concrete arcade of shops which had been the planners' only concession to providing for the residents. Most of the shops had been boarded up or were encased behind bars and grilles. The probation office was reached through a door defaced by graffiti, up some malodorous concrete steps. It was over a fish-and-chips shop. The waiting room was empty except for one fat old lady who drank cider from a dirty brown bottle, and who was dressed despite the sun in layers of clothing. Three middle-aged typists sat on the other side of a strengthened glass window and talked about their holidays.

The senior probation officer was named Joanna and was, it seemed, willing to talk to Molly. No approach had yet been made to her by the police about Greg and Rosco. Claire Bingham had decided that she might talk more freely to a retired social worker than to a policeman about her former clients. Joanna was capable, friendly, in her mid-thirties. Molly thought she would be supportive, accessible, but a little weak. Her staff would take advantage of her. She greeted Molly with something approaching relief. It was pleasant to have a visitor who did not demand money, who spoke in a soft, well-educated voice, whose first enquiries were vague, almost academic. The office was at the back of the building and looked out not over the shopping arcade but over an asphalt children's play area with one vandalised swing. It was similar to many Molly had visited before she retired. There was the same scratched green filing cabinet, the old Snoopy poster, the shrivelled pot plants.

Molly explained that she had been a social worker and that she was there on behalf of the Franks. She was vague about her actual relationship with Greg's parents but stressed their shock and confusion over their son's death.

"I'm sorry," Joanna said. "I'm not sure I can help." She gave an automatic reassuring smile.

"After such a violent and sudden death," Molly said, "I'm sure you can see that it would help the grieving process if they knew more about his life. It would give them something to hang on to.''

The probation officer nodded sympathetically. They were professionals together sharing the same jargon, the same detached quality of professional understanding.

''When did Greg Franks appear in court?'' the senior asked.

Molly told her.

''We've had a big turn round in staff since then. You might find someone who remembers him, but I doubt it. We wouldn't have anything here in writing. You say that he pleaded not guilty to the burglary charge. It's not this office's policy to do social enquiry reports on not-guilty pleas. Besides, I'd not be able to show you anything official like that anyway.''

''No,'' Molly said. ''Of course not.'' She paused. ''Don't you remember him?'' she asked. ''He was in the probation hostel for a couple of months while he was on bail. I know you were on maternity leave for most of the time, but you must have been back at work, I think, before he went to trial. You were back at work, weren't you, before the fire?''

''How did you know about that?'' Joanna was a little suspicious but not too concerned.

''Oh,'' Molly said absently, ''Greg must have mentioned it to his parents.''

Yes, the senior said. She was back by then. But she hardly had time to get to know all the residents before they were all dispersed. The fire had left the hostel uninhabitable. It had been a dreadful time. There had been an enquiry, a lot of media fuss about safety standards. Luckily the enquiry had found that none of the probation officers had been to blame, but it had been a worrying time.

''You were in the hostel on the night of the fire?'' Molly asked.

''Yes,'' she said rather sharply, ''though I don't know what that has to do with the business now. It was my sleeping-in duty.''

''And you really don't remember Greg Franks?'' Molly

said. "He would have been young, rather cocky. His parents claim he was something of a hero at the fire."

Joanna shook her head. "I'm sorry," she said. "I don't remember."

"What about Louis Rosco?" Molly asked. "He was in the hostel at the same time as Greg."

But the senior seemed to have lost her enthusiasm for the conversation.

"I don't know," she said. "It was a difficult time for me. A new baby. Not much sleep. It all seems rather a blur now."

Suddenly she seemed very eager to have the office to herself. She looked at her watch.

"The rest of the team will be having their tea break soon. Why don't you join them? You might find someone who remembers the men you're asking about and be prepared to talk to you informally."

She lifted the telephone and asked the receptionist to take Mrs. Palmer-Jones to the tearoom.

"Make her welcome and give her all the help she needs," Joanna said, and the automatic smile returned.

The tearoom was small and cramped, with a selection of ancient armchairs marked by cigarette burns and coffee stains. The window was tiny and protected by a metal grille, so an electric light burned continually. The room filled quickly with men and women. None, it seemed, had any qualms about helping her, but no one had any recollection of Greg Franks or Louis Rosco. They told her that if Rosco had been on parole, there must be a record somewhere of his probation officer. And one of them would have prepared a social enquiry report before he was sent away. Had she tried the office in Cornwall? If Louis was still on parole when he moved south, all his records would have been sent there. Molly began to think she had come on a wild-goose chase and settled just to recapture the pleasant memories of her life at work.

She sat in a lumpy old armchair, drinking tea, enjoying the familiar bitchiness of social work conversation. They had given all their energy and generosity to their clients and had no compassion left for their colleagues. They discussed divorce, adultery, and the office power games with relish.

"So you know Jane Pym?" one said to Molly. "She was my supervisor when I did a student placement here. She's a brilliant officer. She taught me an amazing lot! But I can't stand her husband. Talk about arrogant! Have you heard the way he talks to her?" She lowered her voice in an excited whisper. "I wouldn't be surprised, you know, if he didn't beat her up. When I was doing my training here, I'm sure she had a bruised face."

"Nonsense," said another, sensing immediately the opportunity for gossip. "He doesn't beat her up. He might be a sadist with the kids at school, but he wouldn't dare touch Jane. You probably caught her on one of her bad mornings. She'd have had a hangover. I don't know any other woman who can drink like Jane. Don't you remember that party at the Housing Office last New Year?"

Then Molly was entertained by all the old stories which must have been repeated every time there was an audience. She was told about the senior who was so drunk that he tripped down the witness stand steps on his way to give evidence in court, about the local police superintendent who dressed up in women's clothes, about the parties they attended so they could at last forget clients and enjoy themselves.

She could have stayed all day listening to the warmth of their conversation, but they began slowly to drift away and back to work. She was thinking that she would have to admit defeat and leave, too, when the door was pushed open to reveal a probation officer who had been in court. His arms were full of files, and he stood for a moment helplessly, then tipped them in a heap on an empty chair. He was prematurely middle-aged, balding, with little round spectacles. His suit was crumpled and poorly fitting and was obviously only brought out for the days when he was on court duty. On his feet were brown suede desert boots.

By now only the typists were left in the tearoom. Three of them sat in a row, knitting. They wore almost identical

153

blouses and cotton skirts. One looked up briefly as the man came in.

"Mike," she said, "This is Mrs. Palmer-Jones. She's looking for someone who remembers Greg Franks or Louis Rosco. Jo says we should help her."

He poured stewed tea from a big brown pot, blinked, and looked at Molly.

"I remember Louis Rosco," he said. "I did the original social enquiry report, visited him a couple of times in prison, and supervised him on parole for a couple of months when he first came out. I expect the papers were transferred to Cornwall. He came from there. He won't be on parole now, though. It would have ended ages ago."

In time with each other, like the chorus of a musical, the typists speared wool with knitting needles, sighed loudly, and stood up. They filed in a line out of the room. Molly almost expected them to return and curtsey.

"What was he like?" Molly asked.

"Why do you want to know?"

"Louis is being held by the police in Cornwall in connection with a murder. As far as I can see, the only reason for his arrest is that he met the victim, Greg Franks, at a probation hostel here. I'm not convinced Louis had anything to do with it."

"He never meant to kill that security guard in the boat yard," Mike said. "I saw him in the remand centre before he went to court, and he was really shocked even then. He was angry, too."

"Why was he angry?"

The man paused. "I think there was more to the arson than the police would ever recognise," he said. "Officially, at least. I know one of the officers on the case had his suspicions about it, too, but he couldn't persuade anyone else to take them seriously." He looked at Molly through his thick spectacles. "I went into a lot of detail to prepare the original social enquiry report," he explained. "More than I'd have time for now. I was just out of college. He was the first report on a serious crime I'd ever done. That's why I remember the case so well."

"Don't you think Rosco set fire to the boat yard?"

"Oh, yes," Mike said. "He admitted that as soon as he was arrested. But I think he'd been paid to do it. By his boss. Only his boss didn't tell him about the security guard who paid routine visits to the premises throughout the night."

"Why should anyone want to set fire to his own boat yard?"

"For the insurance money," Mike said. Later, when she was to discuss this with Claire, Molly thought it significant that Mike had come so close to the truth. He did not have the details about Barnes, but they agreed that Rolfe's version of events was confirmed and strengthened by the probation officer's own enquiries at the time of the crime.

"Why didn't Rosco tell the police that he'd been paid to start the fire?"

"Perhaps he's not that sort of man. Perhaps he was threatened. Or perhaps the plan all along was that he should be caught and convicted—the insurance company would have to pay up then—but he was well paid for the time spent inside."

The *Jessie Ellen*, Molly thought. The payment for keeping his mouth shut was the *Jessie Ellen*.

"Did you suspect that Rosco had anything to do with drugs?" Molly asked.

Mike shook his head. "I can't imagine there'd be anything like that." he said. "According to everyone who knew him, he was quiet, respectable, hardworking. I found him hard to talk to. He only showed any animation when he was discussing boats. He wanted to go back to Cornwall. That was his plan all along."

"When you supervised him on parole, did you meet any of his friends?" Molly asked.

"No," the man said. "We didn't get close at all. He saw the parole commitment as a formality. He reported to the office when I asked him, but he gave nothing of himself away."

"He never mentioned Greg Franks to you?"

"No," Mike said. "I don't remember that name." He stood up awkwardly. Molly supposed he had other clients to see. "Work," he said. "If you see Louis Rosco, send him my best wishes. I regret sometimes that I never persuaded him to tell me what happened at the boat yard. I was inexperienced; I feel that I've let him down." He shook her hand, and she could imagine his having made the same gesture of sad formality when he sent Rosco home to Cornwall.

Molly began to make her way out of the building to the street. She walked down the long corridor towards reception and noticed that the senior probation officer's door was open. She hesitated at the door, thinking that she should thank Joanna, say goodbye. But the woman was writing a report with intense concentration and seemed not to notice that Molly was there.

It was almost lunchtime, and when she went outside, the shopping centre was busier. The chip shop was open, and a straggle of people stretched onto the pavement. Near the launderette there was a group of mothers with bin bags of washing perched on prams and pushchairs. They reminded each other optimistically that the kids would be back at school in a couple of days, and then they could have some time to themselves again.

"But at least it's been fine," they said, looking at the sky, where the wispy trails of cloud were becoming more substantial. "At least they haven't been in under our feet for six weeks." They were cheerful. Now that the holidays were almost over, they could laugh at the ordeal.

They took no notice of Molly standing, bemused, in the centre of the arcade. She was a scruffy little lady who might have come from the old people's sheltered housing on the edge of the estate. When she took out an *A to Z* and studied the road map, the women thought she could be a social worker or someone from Educational Welfare checking that the regular truants were prepared for school.

Molly looked up the Pyms' address in the index and then found the map. They lived in an area of the city which she would have to pass on her way back to the hospital.

There was time to walk back, she thought, and she could make a detour past the Pyms' house, just out of curiosity. She needed the exercise and the time to consider all she had learned in the probation office. She set off down the windy main street towards the town centre, pausing occasionally to study the map. As her surroundings became more respectable, she recalled the events on the *Jessie Ellen*, given greater significance by the information she had learned about Greg and Louis. In a smart suburban shopping street, which might once have been a village high street, she stopped suddenly.

"Of course," she said to herself. "Of course."

The well-dressed women with their designer carrier bags watched her with sympathy and fear. Community care was all very well, they thought, but it let such odd characters onto the streets!

Unaware of their mistrust, Molly trudged on.

The Pyms lived in a solid Edwardian terrace not far from the high street. Molly walked slowly past the house, and while she did not actually limp, managed to convey that her pace was the result of arthritis, not undue curiosity. Now that she was here, the detour seemed a waste of time. She would discover nothing from the neat front lawn or the grey stone walls of the house. She was looking at the map again to find the quickest way back to the hospital when a woman came out of the house next to the Pyms' and called to her.

"Excuse me," she said. "You're not the woman who's come to look at the house, are you? The estate agent said they might be sending someone. The For Sale sign isn't up yet, but I can show you round if you like."

"Please," Molly said. "That would be very kind."

"I don't want to leave really," the young woman chattered as she opened the door into the front room. "We've only just got it straight. My husband's a do-it-yourself freak. He's not really happy unless he's doing up a house. But look at this new kitchen. I'd really miss the ceramic tiles. Would you like some coffee? I'll make some when I've shown you upstairs."

Molly said she would and waited patiently until the tour of the house was completed. She marvelled at the fitted wardrobes, the rebuilt bathroom, the extra bedroom in the loft. Only when they were sitting in the gleaming streamlined kitchen did she ask about the woman's neighbours.

"What are they like?" she said, sipping instant coffee.

157

"Neighbours can make so much difference to settling into a new home. Especially in a terrace."

"I know what you mean," the woman said. "We had teenagers at twenty-eight until recently, playing the saxophone all night. But you're all right. They've gone to college now, and they don't even seem to come home for the holidays."

"What about the people in thirty-two?" Molly asked. The Pyms lived at thirty-two. "Do you get any trouble from them?"

"She's all right," the woman said, the urge to gossip stronger than the desire to sell the house. "*She*'s very quiet. Always polite but keeps herself to herself. Sometimes I wonder if she's got some illness. Something progressive that develops early. She always looks so pale, and a couple of times I've been to the doctor's and seen her in the waiting room."

The woman seemed afraid that as soon as she moved, Jane Pym would make public her life-threatening illness, and she would be denied the drama of it and the satisfaction of telling people that she had known all along.

"What about the husband?" Molly asked. "What's he like?"

"He's a teacher," the woman said; then again discretion was overwhelmed by her pleasure in a good story. "But he's got a dreadful temper."

"Oh?" Molly said, the ideal audience, wanting more.

"Terrible," the woman said, and Molly thought that the Bristol accent was perfect for gossip, soft, confiding, friendly. "Last year we creosoted our fence. Roger Pym stormed round here late one night and accused us of killing all the plants in his garden. You could see it wasn't true, but there was a dreadful scene. I thought I'd have to get the police, but he went quietly enough in the end. His wife made him see sense. We haven't had much to do with him since then, but"—she paused to heighten the dramatic effect—"one of the neighbours says he killed their cat, strangled it with his bare hands, just because it was taking the birds coming onto their bird table. I knew when we first moved in that he was

158

weird.'' She lowered her voice and said in a shocked whisper, ''He's a grown man, and he goes birdwatching!''

Soon after, Molly left. She thanked the woman for showing her around. She had other properties to see, she said. She was very impressed with the new kitchen but thought she might find it a little intimidating. She had enjoyed the conversation. It had really been very interesting.

In the hospital Molly and Claire found George still in bed but desperate to leave. He was a fractious and unhelpful patient, and the staff would have been pleased to be rid of him, too.

''This is ridiculous!'' He was raging to the staff nurse who was trying to take his pulse. ''You've seen the X rays. You know there's nothing broken. So why do I have to wait for the doctor?''

''You've had a concussion and serious bruising,'' she said. ''Besides, I'm not supposed to have given you the results of the X rays.''

''This is madness!'' he cried. ''I should be in Cornwall. There are things I should do.''

He did not tell her that he had heard a gale warning through the radio earphones which hung round his neck like a stethoscope. Hurricane Erin had already hit parts of the Republic of Ireland and was expected over the south-west peninsula after dark.

Claire Bingham took them back to Cornwall. George was in no fit state to drive, and he felt that his nerves were already too frayed to suffer Molly's speed and erratic braking. They left their car outside Gwen Pullen's house, deciding it would be easy to get a train back to Bristol, and that they could collect it then.

In the car he listened to the women talking about the fire at the Sinclair yard, the lurking and sinister presence of Barnes, and the domestic habits of Roger and Jane Pym. At first he found it hard to make sense of the mass of detail. The connection between Greg Franks, Louis Rosco, and Barnes seemed so complex. Besides, he found it difficult to concentrate. While the women discussed the case, he daydreamed of black-browed albatross. It was only later, when they were

159

crossing the Tamar Bridge that the implication of the women's discoveries struck him.

"You do realise," he said, "that all the work you've done in Bristol gives strength to the idea that Rosco killed Greg Franks. Franks had found out about Barnes' dubious business practise in the development of Rashwood Hall. We know that because he was blackmailing Duncan James about it. If Barnes had become aware that Franks had access to damaging inside knowledge, was even using it to make a profit, he would want him out of the way. He'd used Rosco to do his dirty work once before. Why not again? It's obvious. That must be how it happened."

"No," Molly said. "You haven't been listening. There's another explanation."

Then she told them what must have happened. They listened, and the thing was so obvious and so simple that they wondered how they had never worked it out for themselves.

"Wargan will never accept it," Claire Bingham said. "Not without proof. He doesn't believe in coincidence."

But George thought he could get Wargan his proof, though he said nothing to the policewoman. Despite her new flexibility she might not approve. As they drove through the grey towns of north Cornwall, the sky was cloudy and overcast. When they came to Porthkennan it started to rain.

Vicky Jones stood in the gloom of Temple Meads Station. She had little idea where she would go. It scarcely mattered. George Palmer-Jones' visit and the news of his accident had frightened her. There was nothing in Bristol to keep her now.

13

The storm which first hit Cornwall on the day and night of September third was as strong as the hurricane which devastated the south of England in October 1987, but less was heard of it on radio and television. This might have been because it only touched the west coast of the peninsula and no big centres of population were affected. What interest could most of the country have in a few remote cottages swept away by freak high tides, caravan sites flattened, boats smashed into pieces? Besides, by the time reporters realised the extent of the damage the storm was causing, it was too late to get a film crew there in daylight, and by the next morning the rail link had been broken, and most roads were blocked by fallen trees.

The gale began slowly on the night of September second, the evening of Molly and George's return from Bristol to Myrtle Cottage. The wind was strong enough by then to make a noise in the trees around the house and to excite the birdwatchers staying there, but it was not unusual. There were strong westerlies every September at neap tide. By the next morning the wind was as strong as anyone could remember, and even at the head of the valley it tasted of salt, with spray blown up from the beach. The storm reached its peak at midafternoon of the third at high tide, and then the noise of water and wind was terrifying, and though the seawatching was so magnificent that the birders continued to stagger out to Porthkennan Point, it was a major expedition to walk the few hundred yards to reach there.

When Molly and George were dropped at Myrtle Cottage by Claire Bingham, the others were sitting much as they had been the night before. Walking through the door, the Palmer-Joneses saw exactly the same scene as Berry had seen when he arrived to collect Jane Pym. Molly thought it was possible to believe that no one had moved all day. They had eaten a meal, and there was the same clutter as before—scraps of French bread, the sad remnants of a salad, empty wine bottles.

The only difference was that Louis Rosco was there, too. That surprised George—he had expected him to be still in custody—but it would make things easier. The relationship between Rosco and Rose seemed to have changed. Rose had taken public possession of him, and the new show of friendship had caused a tension in the room. Gerald Matthews obviously hated it and was making himself unpleasant, criticizing everything, trying to provoke argument. At first glance nothing else seemed to have changed. Rob Earl and Roger and Jane Pym sat in their accustomed places, drinking heavily. Duncan James shrank into his seat, quiet, self-effacing, almost forgotten.

The conversation was no longer of the murder and when they might be allowed home. The real birdwatchers were no longer eager to go. They spoke in a series of bird names—Cory's shearwater, great shearwater, bonxie—which was a sort of incantation or prayer for the following day. The wind, Molly thought, provoked the same obsession as the boat trip had done. It was the same madness to do with birds and the sea, and she saw, as soon as they arrived, that George was infected by it, too.

When they walked into the kitchen, there was very little response to their arrival. Molly had expected questions about what they had discovered in Bristol, about George's accident. She thought they would want to know when the enquiry would be finally over, but they seemed to have decided by mutual unspoken consent that Greg Franks should be forgotten. Their lack of concern made her angry. What right had they to decide that Greg's life was of such little value? Roger Pym's only interest was in whether George had managed to discuss the red-footed petrel with Gwen Pullen.

"Did you get to the museum? Did Gwen tell you about the old record of a colony of similar birds on the Aleutian Islands? We should have taken a tape recording of the bird's call, you know. That could be decisive. Did you discuss a name? We really should have a name. ... ."

And he paused, hoping that they would suggest that the bird should be called after him. He had come to believe that the discovery was his, and he would be remembered forever as the person who had identified Pym's red-footed petrel.

So George was brought immediately into the conversation, and Molly marvelled that he could appear so calm and absorbed while she felt such a terrible responsibility.

Later in the evening the doorbell began to ring, and all night there was the sound, hardly discernible against the wind, of cars driving down the valley. The people at the door were birdwatchers who had seen the forecast and wanted to be at Porthkennan Head at dawn. Did Rose have any space? they wanted to know. Could she put them up for the night? They stood on the doorstep in the rain like helpless little boys.

At another time she might have tried to help them, given them floor space to unroll their sleeping bags, invited them in for something to eat. But that night she was in no mood to be hospitable. She even resented the old residents. She wanted Louis Rosco to herself. She felt that at any time he might be taken back to Heanor for questioning, and she was edgy and frightened. She would not leave his side, and often she reached out her hand for reassurance. At last, when half a dozen loads of birdwatchers had stopped to ask for shelter, she took a piece of paper and wrote NO VACANCIES on it and pinned it to the front door. Then they were only disturbed by the headlights shining in at the kitchen window as the birdwatchers drove on down towards the beach, where they slept in their cars.

The constant movement in the lane outside, the thought of strangers in the valley, unsettled Molly, and she felt that the

163

others were restless, too. Jane stood up from the table and wandered to the window to watch the cars. Duncan James played with the napkin on his plate, pleating and turning it in his short, fat fingers. Yet George seemed not to notice. He sat in a huddle with Roger, Rob, and Gerald, mumbling the same list of skuas and shearwaters, excited, it seemed, by no other thought than the seawatching.

That evening in the police station at Heanor Claire Bingham, Berry, and Wargan had a meeting in the superintendent's office. The place was unexpectedly busy. There had been flood alerts, and the station was administrating the evacuation of low-lying villages close to the river. Everyone seemed to be enjoying the drama and change from routine. A pile of sandbags had been delivered into the front office, and members of the public came in a stream to collect them. There was a suppressed excitement and a forced community spirit which gave them a taste of what it must have been like in the war. Wargan pointedly ignored the activity. He shut his door on the noise, implying that they at least had real police work to get on with. Yet despite his irritation at the disruption all around him, Claire found him surprisingly enthusiastic. He even congratulated her on her work.

"You did a good job in Bristol," he said. "You'll make a good detective yet."

She said nothing. Both Wargan and Berry were even more convinced of Rosco's guilt. They, too, had followed George's reasoning. The link with Barnes made it devious, Wargan said. He sat behind his desk beaming with self-satisfaction. It was clear to Claire that he had taken credit for all her discoveries in Bristol. Now he wanted the biggest catch of all—the arrest of Brian Barnes.

"The involvement of Brian Barnes with Greg Franks caused some excitement in Bristol," Wargan said. He was smug, very Cornish. We can teach those city boys a thing or two, he implied. "The serious crime squad has been looking for an excuse to get a closer look at Barnes for a while," he said. "There have been all sorts of rumours of corruption but never any proof. Perhaps now he'll be frightened into

164

making a mistake. A surveillance team will be keeping an eye on him for a few days, and I understand they hope to get authorisation to monitor his phone calls. If they can find a link between Brian Barnes and the Greg Franks murder, we'll be popular. Very popular indeed.''

"Did they find anything in Vicky Jones' flat?'' Claire asked. She had told the detective in Bristol all the information George had discovered. She had left them to talk to Vicky Jones.

Wargan shook his head. "She's skipped,'' he said. "When they got there, she'd already gone.'' He even took satisfaction in this. It indicated an inefficiency on the part of the city police which compared poorly with his own officers. "Has anyone questioned Barnes about George's accident?'' Claire asked.

"No,'' he said. "Even they've got more sense than that. They don't want to frighten him off. Besides, what would be the point? Palmer-Jones didn't even get the make of the car. We could never prove it had anything to do with Barnes.''

"Should we bring in Duncan James?'' Berry said. "It wouldn't be hard to get him to talk.''

But because Wargan was daunted by the technical nature of James' deception, he dismissed it as insignificant. What did a site of special scientific interest mean? It didn't seem much of an offence. He had a sneaking sympathy for the developer. His daughter was in Greenpeace, and he thought they were a bunch of weirdos. He had heard enough about the environment to last him a lifetime.

"Not yet,'' he said. "At least until we've more idea what it's about. If we have him in, Barnes might guess what we've got on him. Leave James to stew. He's harmless enough. He's no danger to anyone.''

"What about Rosco?'' Berry asked.

"Leave him where he is, too. His solicitor was muttering about his rights last night.'' He looked at Claire. "He's one of your husband's mob. Let's leave him for twenty-four hours and wait for Barnes to make a move. If he tries to get in touch with Rosco, we've got them both.''

Then Claire Bingham felt powerless and resentful. The

case had been taken from her and was being run by Wargan and his friends in the serious crime squad in Bristol. While it had been considered an accident, even a domestic murder, she had been allowed to handle it. Now she was being told that she had no further part in it. Wargan began an intolerably chummy phone call to a colleague in Bristol and waved his subordinates away.

Even Berry seemed to think that her opinion no longer counted for anything. When she took him into her office and tried to explain why she thought Rosco was innocent, he listened politely but made it clear that he was unconvinced. It seemed farfetched, he said. He couldn't believe it of a person like that. He, too, had been seduced by the influence of the city policemen, with their advanced technology, and by the very scale of Barnes' crime. He preferred Wargan's explanation—it was more exciting—and he refused to look at the facts.

She told no one at Heanor police station of the details of Molly's theory. She would have felt foolish persisting against such opposition. But she would take great delight in seeing Wargan proved wrong. Instead, she went home to Richard and talked to him.

The first indication that things were wrong was Vicky Jones' disappearance, but in the beginning Brian Barnes was not too concerned about that. An enquiry agent had been snooping around Rashwood Hall asking questions, and Vicky had agreed to talk to him. Naturally she was frightened. Later Barnes found out that she had been living with Greg Franks, and when the relationship became known to him, he was furious. He vowed never to trust a woman again.

Then there were more disturbing signs of a lack of confidence. He had arranged to meet the deputy chief constable at Rashwood Hall for lunch, but when he arrived at his office, there was a hasty message on his answering machine cancelling the appointment. There was no apology or explanation.

The rumours were whispered in person and over the telephone from early morning. They were passed on by employees hoping for money and by businessmen wanting to extricate themselves from new contracts. Rolfe had worked quickly.

"I hear that the case of the fire at Sinclair's yard has been reopened," they said. "Rosco's prepared to talk. He's involved with the death of that lad in Cornwall, and he's done a deal with the police."

The informants were frightened because they knew that they would be affected by Barnes' downfall, but they were pleased, too. No one liked him. He had too much money and too much power. They exaggerated and strengthened the rumours so Rosco became a key witness, essential to the police's case. It was all over for Barnes, they implied. Rosco had done for him.

The sudden isolation and suspicion did not come as a shock. Like Vicky Jones, he knew that success was temporary and precarious. But he was a fighter, and he was not prepared to let it go easily. There was something exhilarating in the danger. He felt younger, and all his senses were sharper. He saw a man in a navy anorak standing outside his office with his back turned to the blustery wind and knew instinctively that he was a policeman. Barnes looked forward, too, to the excuse for violence. Since he had become outwardly legitimate, there had been little opportunity for that, and he realised now that he missed it. In this state of readiness and tension he saw Rosco as his only enemy. If he could prevent Rosco from appearing in any court case against him, he would be safe. Later he was amazed that he considered the thing so simple, but at the time it was the simplicity of the danger facing him which was exciting. The thrill took him back to the gang fights in the dance halls of his youth.

When Barnes made his phone call to Cornwall, no one listened to the conversation. It had taken longer than the police had expected to have the monitoring of his calls approved. The deputy chief constable had, for some reason, not been keen.

Barnes spoke to the housekeeper who cared for his house there. He tried to speak with something of the grace of the landed gentry and imagined himself, as he was talking, in

167

his country uniform of Barbour jacket, hunter Wellingtons, and cloth cap. It reminded him of what he had to lose.

He had a favour to ask, he said. It was rather urgent, or he would not consider troubling her. He knew her husband's business took him to Porthkennan. Could he please take a message to a business contact there?

"Just ask him to phone me," Barnes said. "Tell him it's vital. A matter, actually, of life or death."

Smiling, he replaced the telephone receiver.

As soon as it was light, the birdwatchers emerged from their cars and vans and went onto the low headland to look at the sea. The short grass sloped into fingers of rock, so it was possible with care to climb to the water. There was no shelter on the exposed headland, and they huddled into the rock to get some relief from the wind. Soon it became clear that the night of cramped discomfort, the walk through the cold and wet, had been worth suffering. Thousands of seabirds were blown close to the shore. By nine o'clock they had seen all the species of skua ever recorded in Britain. The birdwatchers squatted in huddles and peered occasionally through binoculars towards the horizon. They shouted above the wind to alert the others to especially exciting birds. By lunchtime they were cold and hungry, but no one dared leave the headland for fear of missing something spectacular. They knew birdwatchers would talk about September third for years. They would be envied for being there.

They were surprised when George Palmer-Jones refused to join them on the headland. He was feeling his age a little, he said. It must have been the accident. If he was feeling stronger, he might join them later. He took a chair into the enclosed front porch of the cottage. Through the glass he had a view down the valley, and he had his binoculars with him. Old George is being a bit optimistic, the birdwatchers said, if he thinks he can seawatch from there. Rose fussed around him and brought a rug to tuck around his knees and cups of tea. Only Molly knew he was tense and alert, and that it was all part of the plan.

The night before, when the others began to go to bed, Rosco had gone back to the cottage on the shore. George had stood up, too, stretched, and offered to walk down the lane with him. He needed the exercise he had said when Rosco seemed surprised. He was stiff after the car journey and could do with the walk. It was very late when he returned to Myrtle Cottage.

On the morning of the storm Rose fretted about Louis and wanted to go to see him.

"It can't be safe," she said. "Look at those waves, and it's not high water yet. He should be up here with us."

But Molly persuaded her to leave him alone.

"Louis knows what he's doing," she said. "If there's really any danger, he'll come back. Besides, you've enough to do here."

That was true. Rose's instinct to mother them all had returned. While Matilda played on a rug on the kitchen floor, she made soup in a vast pan. She thought the birdwatchers on the headland would need feeding when it was all over. So she stood in the kitchen peeling vegetables, pretending that her tears were caused by onion skins or tiredness. But when Molly went in to offer help, the tension was suddenly too much for her.

"The police think Louis killed Greg Franks, don't they?" she cried. "Why don't they arrest him and take him back to Heanor? What sort of game are they playing?"

"It's no game." Molly said.

By late morning it was raining heavily. There was a sudden downpour which flooded the drains and turned the lane into a river. Soon it became clear that even if the police had wanted to get to Porthkennan for Rosco, the journey would have been impossible.

With an echoing crash that might have been thunder, the chimney of the old tin mine at the top of the valley toppled like a pile of children's building bricks, and the road was blocked by rock and rubble. A farmer who lived up the lane brought the news that they were cut off.

"It'll take them days to dig us out," he said with gloomy satisfaction. His Wellington boots spread mud over the

169

kitchen floor. "There's nothing we can do about it. The fall brought the phone lines down, too."

He made them switch on the local radio, and they listened, fascinated, to the stories of wreckage and destruction. All the boats left in Heanor harbour had been smashed against the harbour wall by freak gusts of wind, said a disc jockey, with the same forced jollity with which he announced the latest hit. Rose thought that at least the *Jessie Ellen*, which had been winched up to a slipway while the police scientists tested for traces of heroin, would be safe. That gave her some comfort. The farmer, with his talk of flooded fields and financial disaster, gave her none, and they were glad when he went at last.

In the wind Jane Pym felt closer to Roger than she had for years. As they walked into the full force of it down the headland, Roger put his arm around her and pulled her inside his jacket. She carried his tripod over her shoulder as she had done when they were students. They stumbled together over the flattened heather.

"You don't have to come if you don't want to," he said. "You can wait with Rose if you'd rather. She won't mind."

"No," she said. "I'm enjoying it." In the wild weather the differences between them seemed insignificant, and she felt that they could face any trouble together.

"Look," he said. "There are some things I wanted to tell you. . . ." But by then they had reached the relative shelter provided by the rocky crevices. He was drawn immediately into the nearest huddle of birdwatchers, who wanted to gloat about what they had already seen. He released his grip on her and absently reached out for the tripod, which he began to make secure on a flat slab of rock. The moment of intimacy was lost. She thought she was a fool to have been taken in by it.

For the rest of the day he gave his attention to the admiring birdwatchers, who wanted to hear again the story of the new petrel, and to the sea. She might not have been there, and when she slipped away, he did not notice.

Rob Earl and Gerald Matthews walked together to the

170

headland at first light, before the storm had reached its peak. As they walked past the cars parked at the end of the lane, Gerald twitched disapprovingly and muttered about the irresponsibility of people who should know better. Some had misted windows because the occupants were still sleeping. In others men were climbing stiffly from sleeping bags, swearing at the cold, at Rose Pengelly who had refused to give them shelter in her home.

Rob Earl seemed not to notice the cold. He was wearing a frayed jersey with holes at the elbow and a thin denim jacket but no coat. He had not shaved since he had arrived in Cornwall and looked dark and dirty but rather glamorous. In contrast Gerald, wrapped in coat and scarf, seemed unadventurous, something of an old woman. He spoke, too, in petulant, shrewish bursts.

"I'm not sure I did the right thing in packing in the job with the electronics firm," he said. "Look where I am now! No prospects, no future, not even any friends to speak of. At least if I'd stayed in Wiltshire, there would have been a real income. I'd have been able to afford holidays, a decent car. It's time I settled down. I'm too old for this sort of thing."

Rob Earl was preoccupied. At another time he might have put Gerald down with sharp and haughty sarcasm, but he seemed not even to hear. He stalked on ahead, his telescope already fixed to its tripod, balanced on his shoulder, like some space-age weapon of destruction.

In the bunkroom at Myrtle Cottage Duncan James was preparing to leave. The message from Barnes had been given to him earlier. It had come quite unexpectedly, delivered by the man who brought the milk to the valley and who was the husband of Barnes' housekeeper. The man came to the bunkroom, and when James was alone passed on the message in a stage whisper and with a wink, as if he believed some multimillion-pound deal depended on his discretion. The ridiculous secrecy and the message itself gave Duncan the same symptoms of sweating, breathlessness, and terror as if he had been trapped in a cramped, dark space. He felt he had

171

to escape. With shaking hands he took his clothes and folded them, taking an obsessive interest in the exact geometric shapes they formed, in setting them neatly in the suitcase. In this ritual disposal of his clothes he managed to keep his panic at bay, but as soon as the task was complete, it returned and swamped his reason. He opened the bunkroom door, and the tunnel of wind which swept around the building caught it and banged it against the wall, so he felt that everyone must know he was there. He shut it with difficulty and went into the house. From the kitchen he could hear the familiar clatter of women's voices, and he was reminded of the security of home. He saw George Palmer-Jones, apparently asleep, on the porch, his binoculars unused around his neck. Duncan had an impulse to go to him, to tell him everything, and ask for his help, but the older man's stillness made him unapproachable. Instead, he went quietly to the telephone.

In the conversation with James, Brian Barnes was more persuasive and less gentlemanly than he had been when speaking to his housekeeper. He reminded James of the offences he had already committed, of the big house in Somerset which had been bought largely with Squirrel corporation money. At last he spoke with some brutality of James' children.

"But I couldn't do it," James said. "I wouldn't know where to begin."

"If you're desperate enough, you'll find a way," Brian Barnes said. "And by now you should be desperate."

He replaced the receiver before James could reply, and when James tried to phone Bristol again, it was impossible to get through. Soon after, he heard the farmer stomping into the kitchen with the news that the valley was cut off and the phone lines were down.

The sky was so overcast and the windows of the cottage so small and low to the ground that inside it was almost dark, but Rosco did not bother with the lamps. He sat in the shadow in the old bentwood chair which had once been his father's and waited, his gun cradled like a cat on his knee.

14

By early afternoon Rosco began to realise that whatever he had promised to George Palmer-Jones, it would be impossible for him to remain where he was. It would be dangerous, suicidal. The shingle and boulders which protected the cottage from the water at high tides were already shifting with the force of the waves. The whole beach was creaking, and he imagined the foundations of the cottage moving, as if there had been a earthquake. Besides, he had lost faith in Palmer-Jones. It had been easy to believe him the night before when they had walked down the lane together. It had been flattering to be treated as important by such a respected gentleman, and he had agreed with some pride to George's proposal. Now nothing had happened, and Rosco felt let down. He wanted to be in the warm kitchen in Myrtle Cottage, with the windows misted from the heat of cooking and Rose laughing and the baby on his knees reaching out to touch his face.

He set the revolver carefully on the chair where he had been sitting and began to prepare for evacuation. He had said nothing to George about the revolver. He had obtained it almost by chance from a man he had met in prison soon after his release. He had kept it because he knew instinctively that no one who had ever had dealings with Brian Barnes could consider himself quite safe. He never envisaged himself using it but kept it as a talisman, a charm against evil. In the hours of waiting it had been a comfort. Now, because he no longer believed George's story and thought the only danger he faced would come from the police, he set it aside. He pulled a navy canvas bag from the cupboard under the sink and began to throw things into it. There was not much that he felt worth taking: a favourite jersey which Rose had knitted for him when she was first expecting the baby and which had been airing on a makeshift line in the kitchen, the few important papers he had, an insurance policy, his passport. Then he remembered that there was a photograph of his mother in the drawer in the bedroom, and he went to fetch that.

He did not hear the door of the cottage being opened though he noticed when he was in the bedroom that the noise of the wind had suddenly diminished. The birdwatchers on Porthkennan Head were aware of the moment of stillness, too. Suddenly they could speak to each other without having to shout, and they could breathe more easily. Perhaps it's all over, they said. Perhaps it's blown itself out. But the period of calm was only brief. It lasted perhaps for fifteen minutes; then the storm continued more ferociously than ever. And even when the wind had stopped, the momentum of the waves was unstoppable. It was still not quite high tide, and they fell with relentless power onto the rocks where the birdwatchers were sitting, so the men had to move back onto the grass and set up their telescopes there. Perhaps it was the sound of water which prevented Rosco hearing the door of the cottage being opened, or perhaps he was not sufficiently on his guard. It took him longer than he expected to find the photograph of his mother, but he continued to look because it was inconceivable now that he could leave the house without it. He discovered it at last, without a frame, trapped behind the drawer.

When he went back into the room, the figure, anonymous in anorak and hood and boots, was standing just inside the door, as if only just arrived, but his gun was missing from the chair and was in her hand. He stood across the room from her, still clutching the photograph and thought that Palmer-Jones had been right.

"So it *was* you," Rosco said. "You know, I couldn't remember."

"You wrote me a letter," she said. "It was on my bed last night."

"Yes," he said. "I took a chance, but I wasn't sure."

Jane Pym took down her hood with her free hand, still holding the gun in front of her. Rosco could see that she was finding the revolver too heavy for her hand and that she held her arm rigid, so it was shaking. He had an impulse to tell her that unless she relaxed, she was bound to miss. Instead, he tried to remain calm. He walked back to the chair by the window and saw a wall of grey water break over the boulders nearest to the cottage. If I can keep her talking long enough, he thought, we'll both be drowned. That seemed a more attractive way to die than to be shot by a middle-aged neurotic woman. Only then did he wonder what had happened to George Palmer-Jones and think that he had some responsibility to get at the truth.

"You'd been drinking," he said. "That night of the fire."

"Oh," she said, and she was smiling, "I've always been drinking."

"You should get help," he said.

"Do you think I haven't tried?" she demanded, her voice hard and tense as the arm that held the gun. "I got foul medicine from the doctor which was supposed to make me sick if I had a drink. I stopped taking it. I bared my soul in Alcoholics Anonymous before I realise that half of them were my clients. You don't know."

He did not know. He had no idea what she was talking about. But he sat by the window, inviting her to continue, waiting for the water to sweep them both away.

"Greg Franks recognised you," he said.

"Oh, yes," she said bitterly. "He recognised me. And that was partly my fault, wasn't it? If I hadn't said I thought I'd seen him before, he might have taken no notice. But he recognised me, and he tried to blackmail me. He sat on the deck, still green and seasick, and asked me for money."

"So you hit him and threw him overboard?"

"It didn't happen like that," she cried. "It wasn't planned.

175

But he was grinning, teasing me. 'Still like a drink,' he said, 'don't you? I saw you last night. If I hadn't been at the hostel four years ago, someone might have died.' "

"Was that true?" Rosco was suddenly interested.

"Probably," she said. It no longer mattered to her. "I was sleeping so heavily that I didn't know what was going on. I suppose I was drunk. Franks got everyone else out and then came back for me."

She seemed lost in her memory of the past. The gun jerked suddenly.

"I shouldn't have been there," she said. "I'd finished my contract at the hostel the month before. My friend was the warden. She was back from maternity leave, and it was her turn to sleep in. She phoned me up that day and begged me to do it for her. She couldn't leave the baby, she said. It was teething and screamed all night. She couldn't trust her husband not to strangle it. So I went in as a favour to her. It wasn't my fault."

He was not listening. He was mesmerized by the movement and closeness of the water. He had always thought it was the boats which attracted him and had caused all his trouble, but perhaps it was the sea after all. He waited with a sort of resigned anticipation for the water to come.

"You shouldn't have tried to blackmail me, too," she said sharply, demanding suddenly his attention. "That's what the letter was about, wasn't it?"

"I suppose it was," he said. He had written the letter to George's dictation and had taken little notice of the words.

He could tell that his vagueness and lack of concern irritated her. He wondered what he could say to please her, but there was a jerk and then the noise of gunshot, immensely loud in the enclosed space of the room. It came as an awful surprise to them both. He never knew if she meant to fire the gun, but he could see that she was angry to have missed him. It was another failure.

"No one blackmails me," she said, and he knew then that she meant to kill him.

He turned to look at the water again, thinking that even if he was shot, he could be watching the sea at the same time.

The next wave was so big that it reached the walls of the cottage, and the spray ran down the glass of the window. The silence inside the room surprised him, and a little reluctantly he turned back to face the woman. The scene which met him was so unexpected that he stared dazed and openmouthed, and he could do nothing to help. He watched the cottage door open and George Palmer-Jones appear suddenly behind her. She had straightened her arm to fire again, but George reached out one long and powerful hand and clamped it around the chamber of the revolver. So, although she pulled again and again at the trigger the chamber containing the cartridges could not revolve, and there was no bullet in the barrel to be fired.

The scene took place in silence. It was only when she seemed to realise that with George's hand around the gun she was quite powerless that she screamed. She released her hand from the grip and her finger from the trigger, and with her arms at her sides she shouted at them both, a stream of loud and furious oaths. George went to the open door and flung the gun into the churning waves, then turned back to them, astounded by their stupidity.

"Come on!" he shouted. He seemed the only person with the wit to move. Rosco was still staring, bewildered. "The walls won't hold much longer. We've got to move." Then, directly to Louis, he added, "Rose will never forgive me if anything happens to you."

The mention of Rose's name seemed suddenly to release Rosco from his trance. He picked up the canvas bag and walked across the room to the door. He passed within inches of the woman who had tried to shoot him, but she took no notice and stood quite still, her face in her hands. Outside there was still little wind, but as he waited, a huge wave swept over one of the birdwatcher's cars which had been parked on the shore. It was turned on its side, as if it were a toy. Now is was Rosco's turn to urge hurry.

"Look out," he said. "We'll have to go."

George pulled on Jane's arm and dragged her to the cottage door.

"Leave her," Rosco said. "She's not worth it."

177

Another wave, bigger than any they had seen before, was being funnelled between the headlands. George tried to pick up Jane in his arms like a child, but she kicked out and struggled free. Rosco caught hold of the sleeve of George's jacket and pulled him up the footpath to the higher ground under the trees.

The wave broke over the cottage with a force which ripped out the chimney and tore a hole in the roof. As it was sucked back across the beach, it pulled rock and stone, pieces of furniture, and the whole pile of freshly sawn logs with it. The wood bounced on the surface.

"Where's Jane Pym?" George asked.

"In there," Rosco said, nodding. "She never meant to come out." He felt a vague irritation of envy. It was the way he had chosen to die.

"I'll have to look," George said.

"Don't be a fool. What are you? Some sort of martyr? It's not high water yet."

Then, as if to confirm his words, the wind returned and caught them off balance. With their hoods low over their faces to protect them from broken branches and blowing debris, they walked together back to Myrtle Cottage.

"I'll have to tell Roger Pym," George said when they had almost reached the house.

Rosco paused, gasping for breath. "Do you think he'll care?" he said. "He's so wrapped up with those bloody birds. Do you think he'll even notice?"

Dusk came early that afternoon. As at last the wind quietened, a wet heavy mist came in from the sea. In the fog seawatching was impossible, and all the birdwatchers from the headland wandered inland. For the first time they saw the smashed windscreens and buckled metal of the cars. They took no notice of the shell of the cottage on the shore. That had nothing to do with them. Yet even those whose cars had been damaged maintained their high spirits. They giggled, as if they were high on drink or drugs. It had been such a magnificent day on the headland. They had seen so many birds. They struggled back up the footpath to the lane shouting their good humour.

Some began singing. At the head of the procession Roger, Gerald, and Rob walked arm in arm, their conflicting personalities made unimportant by the shared experience. Only when they got into the house did Roger remember Jane. Then he called out for her, irritated because she wasn't there to greet him, wanting to boast of his triumph in front of her.

15

The full story was not told in detail until Jane Pym's inquest, and then little of the background came out in court. The real inquest took place in the evening. Claire Bingham surprisingly had offered to put George and Molly up for the night. She knew George would be a witness at the hearing, and it would be a pleasure, she said, to have them to stay.

She greeted them at the door of her smart new house like old friends. Molly was afraid she might have bored her husband by talking about them. Certainly Claire seemed very pleased to have them there and had made a great effort to entertain them well. She had dressed in an obviously expensive outfit, but Molly in her second-hand Oxfam dress felt more at ease. They sat behind the large plate glass window and looked down at the harbour, where the lights were beginning to come on and were reflected in the water. There was still evidence of the day of the storm—makeshift repairs to the harbour wall and the lifeboat station in ruins—but on a calm evening the destruction was almost decorative. Claire brought them large drinks and in a brittle, rather self-conscious way talked about her husband's work and the antics of the baby. Berry, who had been invited for a meal, arrived late and then sat quietly in a corner watching her with sympathy and some concern.

It was only later, when they were eating, that Claire told them she had decided to leave the police force. It would never work, she said. She was not suited to it. Molly, with an honesty and persistence which was the result of alcohol and which she would regret in the morning, told her she was a fool. The police force needed women like Claire, she said. How could she allow herself to be beaten by a bunch of ignorant men? By then Molly had drunk more wine than she was used to and became heated and emotional. It was a cop-out, she said. A terrible cop-out. But Claire was not to be persuaded.

Berry sipped mineral water and watched his boss sadly. Richard, the husband, was more sympathetic than Molly had expected. He had not wanted Claire to leave the police, he said in a quiet aside when Molly at last stopped ranting about women's masochistic self-denial. He felt rather guilty about it. He knew he should have given her more support. But she was quite determined, and nothing he could say would make her change her mind. He was not sure how they could manage with only one income.

When they finished the meal, they took coffee back to the living room, and then the real reason for the invitation was clear.

"I want to know exactly what happened on the *Jessie Ellen*," Claire Bingham said. "And how you knew Jane Pym murdered Greg Franks. You never really explained."

Then George thought that by discovering who had killed Greg, they, not Richard Bingham, were responsible for Claire's resignation from the police force. She considered herself a failure because they had come to a successful conclusion before she did. She was ambitious and competitive, and she refused to be beaten. She would rather leave her job than be second-best.

"A lot of luck," he said. "And after all, we were there. . . ."

Molly, less sensitive to Claire's feelings, was willing to boast.

"It was obvious that the murder wasn't premeditated," she said. "How could it have been? Anyone who knew about the pelagic trips would know that in most circumstances Greg Franks would have been out on deck surrounded by people.

181

How could anyone know in advance that he would be seasick? The idea was impossible."

"But why Jane Pym?" Claire asked.

"She was a boozer," Molly said. "We all knew that in the time we spent with her, and it was confirmed by her colleagues in the probation office. She was desperately unhappy. All she had was her job. When he recognised her as the warden of the hostel, Greg Franks threatened that."

"But how did you know she was at the hostel on the night of the fire? All the records showed that she'd left by then."

"It was an intelligent guess," Molly said. "Jane was uneasy all the time in Myrtle Cottage. She was a friend of the woman who was supposed to be in the hostel, her senior. When I met the senior in the probation office, she was obviously anxious and defensive about something. Besides, there were few other people who could have killed Greg. Jane wasn't a serious birder. Anyone who was would have been much more concerned about seawatching than committing murder."

"You make it sound very easy!" Berry said sarcastically.

"It was easy!" Molly said, stretching in her chair, reaching for another drink.

"Nonsense!" George said sharply. "It wasn't easy at all. There was all that complication with Duncan James and Brian Barnes. I was taken in by that, too. The assault outside Vicky James' flat made me personally involved, and I was furious about the Rashwood development." He looked at Claire. "Has anything come of that?"

"Yes," she said. "Barnes is in custody. He's being investigated by the fraud squad. When the rumour that he was in trouble and that Rosco was prepared to testify against him became commonplace, it's surprising how many other members of his staff, quite senior members, came forward wanting to give information against him. They're afraid that they'll be charged, too, and want to make sure that he takes the blame. There are a lot of scared little rats leaving a sinking ship."

There was a silence. They watched a large fishing boat move out of Heanor harbour towards the open sea.

"What will happen to Duncan James?" Molly asked.

"We're not charging him," Claire Bingham said. "We've no proof that he falsified the environmental impact assessment which allowed the development of Rashwood Hall. There might be a way of proving that Barnes passed considerable sums of money into his account, but Barnes was good at covering his tracks. Greg Franks was the only person who knew that Rashwood Park was better for wildlife than Duncan James reported, and he's not here to give evidence."

"It was Duncan James who threw all Franks' gear overboard when he was missing on the *Jessie Ellen*," George said. "That's why Duncan took so long when he went to tell Greg about the petrel. He knew that Greg had kept records of all the birds he had seen at Rashwood. He didn't have time to look through the papers and notebooks properly, so he threw everything away.

"And he won't be prosecuted?" Molly said. "Nothing will happen to him?"

"I think he'll have to resign from the Nature Conservancy Council," George said. "He'll have lost his credibility, though I'm sure he's been so frightened that he would never do anything similar again. Brian Barnes phoned him, you know, on the day Jane Pym died. Barnes said he was having problems with Rosco, and he expected Duncan to sort him out. As if a man like that would have a chance against Rosco. Duncan was terrified. Barnes made threats against his wife and children, and by then the phone lines were down, so Duncan couldn't check that they were safe." George remembered James' hysterical confession on the day of the storm. It had distracted him from his watch on the shore cottage and had almost caused another tragedy. "Duncan will have to live with himself." he said. "And with that monstrous development almost on his doorstep."

There was another pause.

"I don't understand why Jane Pym showed her hand." Berry spoke quietly. He had taken so little part in the conversation that the words surprised them. "Why did she go to Rosco's on the day of the storm? If she'd kept quiet, no one could have proved her guilt."

"Rosco was at the hostel at the same time as Franks," George said, "though he was so wrapped up in his plans for the *Jessie Ellen* that he didn't notice Greg or Jane Pym. He was there on the night of the fire. When we suspected that Jane had killed Greg Franks, I asked Rosco to write to her. The letter said he recognised her as the warden of the hostel, so he knew why Greg had died. She presumed that Rosco was blackmailing her and was so distraught by then that she decided to confront him about it."

"But what could she hope to do?" Claire Bingham said. "She couldn't expect to kill him, too."

"She was very irrational," George said vaguely. "I don't think she had any plans."

He did not say that Rosco had come close to death. Throughout the investigation which had followed Jane Pym's death he had said nothing about Rosco's revolver. Louis had been through enough, he thought. He was entitled to the opportunity to start a new life with Rose and Matilda without more questions from the police. Even Molly knew nothing about the gun.

They looked at each other. Richard Bingham came round again with the wine, and George noticed that as Berry took a glass of fruit juice, there was a moment of disapproval or perhaps complacence. Was he thinking that alcohol had been Jane Pym's downfall? That she was a wicked woman because she had succumbed to the demon drink? George knew that it was all more complicated than that.

The telephone broke the silence, and there was a sudden relief because they no longer knew what to say to each other. Claire Bingham went to answer it and returned almost immediately.

"It's for you," she said to George and smiled flirtatiously. "It's a woman."

The woman was Gwen Pullen, apologetic and enthusiastic at the same time, rather loud.

"I'm sorry to trouble you, George," she said. "It took a lot of detective work to track you down actually. But I thought you'd want to know. I've just come back from Amsterdam. I've been sorting through a pile of skins at the museum.

There was one that they never identified. They always thought it was a sort of aberrant mutation. It was a petrel, actually, with red feet.''

She paused, expecting some response from George, and when none came, she continued: "The bird was remarkably well documented, and this is the most exciting thing. It was donated to the museum by an ordinary seaman who had sailed with a British explorer. I've checked everything out, and he was on the Aleutian Islands expedition. He must have been a better shot than the Englishman, don't you think? The seaman's name was Damus, which has rather a ring to it. So, if everything is approved by the appropriate bodies, I suggest that your bird is known as Damus' petrel. . . . George? Are you there?''

George, who had been holding the receiver away from his ear to prevent himself from being deafened, said that he was there. And he liked the name Damus' petrel, too.

About the Author

The daughter of a village school teacher, ANN CLEEVES lives in Northumberland, England, where she spends her time with her two small children and writing.

SEA FEVER is her latest novel featuring bird watcher sleuth George Palmer-Jones. Her other novels featuring Palmer-Jones are A BIRD IN THE HAND, COME DEATH AND HIGH WATER, MURDER IN PARADISE, and A PREY TO MURDER. She is also the author of MURDER IN MY BACKYARD and A LESSON IN DYING featuring detective Stephen Ramsay.

ANN CLEEVES
writes mysteries
like you've
never read before!